MR. WHISKEY

TESSA LAYNE

I knew she was sin in stilettos the second I laid eyes on her...

But did that stop me? Hell, no.

Because I'm nothing, if not a risk taker. And Roxi Rickoli, with a snake tattoo climbing up her leg and hinting at unparalleled pleasure, tempts me like the devil himself.

And while I can't get enough of the wild redhead who runs my bar, I know that fate is a cruel mistress. And when she comes calling, someone must pay...

Sign up for my newsletter at www.tessalayne.com/newsletter to receive updates, sneak-peeks, and freebies!

Chapter One

*S*ome people call me a fixer. Others call me a dealmaker. Really, I'm just an asshole with a fuckton of money. And tonight I aim to throw Grover Clevelands around like they're candy, not discontinued notes.

My phone buzzes as I pull into the long square drive of the Nelson-Atkins Museum of Art, and drop my keys in the valet's hand. *You're late. We're waiting in Kirkwood Hall.*

"Is that a…" The young man's eyes go round as he stares at my convertible Lotus.

"It is, and no you can't take it for a spin." My cell phone buzzes again. *Are you coming?*

The only reason I let Muffy Templeton talk me into releasing my inaugural cask reserve at tonight's Picasso wing fundraiser for the Nelson-Atkins Museum of Art is because her mother was bosom friends with my great-grandmother. That, and her husband Robert has no problem losing part of his fortune every week at The Whiskey Den.

I smell Muffy before I see her, drenched in her signature lilac scented perfume and dripping in diamonds. "Darling. You must hurry. The guests will be arriving in less than thirty minutes."

I kiss her wrinkled cheek, biting back a sharp retort. Instead, I wink at her. "You worry too much. I promised I'd be here."

She pats my cheek like I'm her son. "It's a good thing you're so handsome, Danny Pendergast."

She's not wrong. My looks and my charm have taken me much farther than the Pendergast name, not that it means much anymore. My great-grandfather might have been the stuff of legends, but his legacy lives on only in the mystique of a bygone era.

Muffy takes my elbow, leading me into Kirkwood Hall, which has been transformed into something out of the twenties, complete with a bandstand in the corner with an old-fashioned microphone. "I found someone to help you for the first hour. Once the whiskey's out, I hope you'll stay and mingle."

I nod, hoping the 'help' isn't her fumble-fingered grandson like it was the last time I let myself get talked into helping Muffy with one of her garden parties. Or worse, the granddaughter she's been trying to set me up with for the past two years. Don't get me wrong, I've enjoyed more than my fair share of debs — eager young women bored with college frat-boys and looking for a real man. One who deals in orgasms and no-strings-attached fucks. And there will be plenty of pussy here tonight, but I've got bigger fish to fry this evening. Muffy has pulled out all the stops for this fundraiser, and fully half of tonight's attendees hail from every major city in the country. High stakes poker, even for a cause, is irresistible to those caught in its web. I should know, it's what brought my great-grandfather to his knees.

Tom Pendergast might have spent his last days under a cloud of shame, but the fact he did hard time only adds to his legendary mystique. All you have to do is stroll through the Crossroads and count the distilleries and bars with his name on them. Me? I choose to honor my great-grandfather in a more... apropos manner. Helping damsels in distress, not asking too many questions about where the cash for my exorbitant membership fees come from. Building relationships with influencers in both the underworld and the business world, because it's funny, how often the two seem to be one and the same. But as long as my money keeps rolling, I don't give a shit. And tonight, the Whiskey Den will be hopping. I've made sure the word has quietly gone out to a few key members that a private, high-stakes game will take place after midnight. So as much as I'd like a tryst in a darkened corner away from the security cameras, I need to bring my A-game.

But one look at my *help's* backside has me regretting the choice to leave the condoms by the bedside table. I don't know what to appreciate first, the arc of her spine that flares into wide hips, or the long red hair that cascades to the middle of her back in thick waves. It takes a second to register she's carrying two boxes of booze-filled flasks, Muffy's idea to send my whiskey home with every guest tonight. I curse, and hurry to take the boxes. "Here. Let me."

I step around her and slip my arms underneath hers. The electricity when we touch is instant. Fire races under my skin, heating my blood.

Her gaze meets mine with a hint of amusement. "I've got it, thanks."

She's not beautiful in the cover-model sense, but she's arresting, and utterly unforgettable. High cheekbones highlight sparkling amber eyes. Her mouth is full and wide —

the kind of mouth that men fantasize about wrapped around their cock — and it pulls into a smile I can't help but return. I gently take the boxes, regretting only that we're no longer touching. "I wouldn't be a gentleman if I let you carry those." I set first one, then the other on a pair of high-tops and begin pulling flasks.

She joins, me, removing flasks from the second box. "I appreciate your chivalry and all, but—"

"Lemme guess, you've got it?" I turn to face her, but the remaining words die in my mouth when I catch sight of the snake tattoo crawling up and around her right leg, bared thanks to the insanely high slit in her black glittery dress. My mouth goes dry as I take in the rest of her front side. She's tall, nearly my height in her stilettos, which makes her five-ten, maybe five-eleven in bare feet. Her tits are like sirens, full and lush under the fabric stretched tight across them. My neck heats as I force my eyes to hers, because holy fuck, this woman could make a living as a goddamned pinup girl.

"I was going to say, I don't need rescuing," she tosses back, still amused, and extends her hand. "Roxi."

I take hers, perversely pleased at the grip that's as strong as my own. This is no damsel in distress, and it's sexy as fuck. "Danny. I brought the booze."

Her smile grows, and she makes no move to loosen her hand. "Ahh. Mr. Whiskey."

"Sure. You can call me that." Every cliché come-on runs through my head. I clear my throat. "Why don't you set up the flasks, I'll grab the rest of the boxes."

"Already done." She points to the other tables near the entrance. "These are just the extras."

"I hope you'll let me buy you a drink later, for your troubles."

"No trouble at all, and maybe."

"You have to let me thank you some way," I offer, not wanting this to be the end of our interaction.

Her eyes smolder as we lock gazes again. In less time than it takes to inhale, I'm hard. Balls tight and aching with need. "I'm sure I can think of something," she answers with a slow grin before turning and gliding away, hips swaying like a snake charmer.

A hand lands on my shoulder. "You might want to put your tongue back in your mouth, pal," says the laughing voice of Harrison Steele low enough that no one else can hear. "I could see the sparks flying between you two from across the room."

I turn to shake his hand. Harrison is one of my oldest friends, and was one of my earliest investors. "I thought you had a date?" My implication is clear — hands off. And it's best to be clear with Harrison, because he considers pussy chasing a sport. And if it was, he'd have won all the Olympic medals. It's hard to blame him, he's got those irresistible All-American good looks — dark hair, blue eyes, and at least according to my bar manager Lisa, a cock that's legendary. Women eat him up like they do pints of Ben & Jerry's. Me? I'm more of an acquired taste — whiskey neat, with a healthy dose of cynicism.

He scowls. "Ditched me."

"No fucking way. Kansas City's most eligible bachelor is flying solo at the gala of the year?"

"Not solo." He winks. "You're going to be my wingman."

"Oh no." I shake my head, grimacing at the memory of the one time I was Harrison's wingman in college. The night did not end well. "I told you I'm never doing that again."

"Aww, c'mon." Harrison claps my shoulder. "How was

I supposed to know that Samantha's friend was dating the president of TKE?"

"Because these are the things you bother to find out when you push your friend into the arms of a strange woman." Thank god the guy was so wasted that when he took his shot, he swung wide, and I was able to drop him with a right hook to the jaw. "Besides, I promised Muffy I'd tend bar until the flasks were handed out."

Harrison rolls his eyes. "Always behind the scenes, pulling strings like a puppet-master. When are you going to let go and start enjoying life?"

I sidestep his question with one of my own. "Where's Stockton?"

"He refused to come tonight because his mother keeps trying to set him up with one of Muffy's granddaughters."

"Stockton's mother has been trying to marry him off since college."

"It's only gotten worse," Harrison states with a scowl. She's taken to 'dropping by the office' with a new girl each week."

"Sounds like you could use a drink," I say, moving to the makeshift bar and filling a tumbler of whiskey directly from the cask. I hand it to him. "Tom's Special Reserve."

He lifts his glass in a toast. "To snatching kisses and kissing snatch."

"Who is she?" I ask, suddenly suspicious. It's not like Harrison to be that crude.

"No one," he answers too sharply.

"Liar. Your eyebrow always twitches when you lie," I say pointing to the corner of his eye. "Whoever she is, she's got you tied up in knots."

Harrison's eyebrows knit together. "The only tying up going on will be happening later tonight."

"But not with Roxi. Just so we're clear," I growl

pouring myself a tumbler. It's not like me to stake a claim, but I've seen Harrison work. He loves the chase almost as much as winning the prize. And I don't know what happened when Roxi and I touched, but I've never felt electrocuted by a woman's touch before. Not like this.

"Roxi, huh? That her name?" Harrison's smile turns sly.

"Don't get any ideas. My love life's off limits."

He spreads is hands. "I just want to help."

"You want to help? Spread the word — discretely — about tonight's poker game."

Harrison quickly turns serious. "What's the buy in?"

"Fifty." He knows I mean thousand. "Limited to the first five. If we have ten, I'll do a second seating at one."

He nods. "See you at midnight?"

Chapter Two

*R*oxi returns pushing a cart of ice. "Who was that?" She nods Harrison's direction.

"Harrison Steele."

"Of Steele Conglomerate?" she confirms with a raised brow.

I nod. "We rowed together at Stanford." I don't know why I volunteer that bit of information, except that I want to flex a bit. I don't row anymore, although not for lack of Steele and the rest of his buddies trying to recruit me. I rowed for connections, not for love of the sport. Steele and his buddies are fanatics.

"What are you doing tending bar tonight, then? Isn't he a co-sponsor?"

Not only is she observant, it's obvious she's done her homework. Or Muffy's prepped her. "Harrison asked if I would provide the booze tonight." I sweep my hand toward the flasks. "Which I have."

She narrows her eyes. "But whiskey makers don't usually bartend?"

I pause, two answers warring in my head. The truth?

I've always been more comfortable behind the scenes. Life experience won't let me *not* work. I wasn't born with a silver spoon in my mouth the way Harrison or Stockton, or the Case brothers were. I had to scrap and fight for everything. And even though now I have everything I could want and more, part of me still feels like it will all go away tomorrow. Like I don't deserve it. But that shit feels way too vulnerable to confess to a stranger, no matter how luscious her curves or how winsome her smile. So I go with the bullshit answer instead. I flash her a smile. "Not unless there's a captivating woman to keep them company."

Her smile broadens. "You think I'm captivating? That makes it sound like you're interested in more than my tits."

I drop my head and laugh. All the way to my toes. There's nothing soft or demure about Roxi, and I fucking love it. She's intelligent too, I can see it in her eyes, in her saucy wit, and that's sexier to me than her curves or the snake crawling up her leg. "Oh I'm definitely interested in your tits." The words hang between us, sparking with electricity. Her gaze heats as my words register. I step into her space. She's practically eye level with me in her stilettos, and I like that too — that I wouldn't have to bend to kiss her, or stoop to fuck her against a wall. My voice turns to gravel. "But I like your mouth more." I can see her absorbing my comment, considering the implication. My heart thunders against my sternum. This feels like a dangerous, sexy game, with stakes higher than the game I'm hosting later tonight, and I'm all in.

"I could totally go for some of you right now," she says in a rush, not looking away. I can feel the heat coming off her in hot waves, the heady floral scent of her filling what little space there is between us. "All of you," she amends.

"You looking for a little naughty time?" I'm shocked we're having this conversation in the middle of the biggest gala of the year. And two-hundred-percent aroused. If we were alone, I'd have her bent over the table in nothing flat, a hand between her thighs. The fact that we can only stare at each other and speak dirty, filthy things quiet enough we're not overheard, is erotic as fuck.

She arches a brow. "I'm looking for a whole lotta naughty."

"Tell me what you want," I say tightly. My cock is like iron, straining so hard against my zipper I swear it's going to have dents. The ache in my balls is painful to the point of distraction, but I can't stop escalating with her. It's too… enticing. My skin feels tight against my bones, hot and itchy. And the only thing that will slake the fire is her touch.

Her voice, when she speaks, sounds strangled, breathless. *Turned on.* "Kiss my neck. Trace my spine. Bite me. Tug my hair. Hold me down. Use your tongue to make me moan."

Holy mother of divine fuck.

"I'll start by tracing that snake tattoo up your leg to where it ends." And I have a very good idea of where it ends. "Would you like that?"

Her pupils are so large her eyes look black. She makes a whimpering noise in the back of her throat and nods imperceptibly.

"And then, when I've reached the mouth of the snake, I'll be damned sure to take my fill of your hot, wet cunt." Her breath is coming in ragged gasps, as if she's halfway to orgasm, sex-drunk on my words alone. It eggs me on. "And only when I've made you come on my tongue, *moaning my name*, at least twice — will I turn you around and take you from behind while I pinch your tight nipples and make you come on my cock." My blood pounds in my ears, hot and heavy with arousal. "That naughty enough for you, Roxi?"

Her tongue slicks her bottom lip, and god, I want to bite her. "It's a start," she says with a smirk.

I'm ready to throw her over my shoulder and go all caveman on her, whiskey flasks and cocktails be damned. But I won't embarrass Steele like that. Or Muffy, who interrupts our stare-down with a snap of her fingers. "Places, darlings. Places. The guests are starting to arrive."

I smile tightly, grateful for the reminder that the last thing I need is an entanglement of any kind. No matter how tempting the lady.

The hour creeps by.

My face hurts from smiling at nameless faces. Beside me, Roxi is the picture of charm, her voice clear and confident as she talks and teases with the guests, offering them tastes from the barrel as they tuck flasks into purses and coat pockets. It's hot, the way she works the crowd like a pro, and it only makes me want to know more about her. "Where did Muffy find you?" I mutter more to myself during a lull.

My answer is full, lusty laughter. Apparently her hearing is razor sharp, too. "I've never met her before tonight," she says, shooting me an amused glance.

I turn and face her. "You're kidding."

She shakes her head, mouth pulling into a saucy grin.

Huh. "And Muffy just recruited you?"

Her smile turns rueful. "I think she might have caught me looking a bit forlorn." She cocks her head, assessing me — as if she's debating how much of herself to reveal. "My date stood me up."

"What the fuck for?" I growl, determined to capitalize on the asshole's loss.

"I can be… a little much," she says with a soft laugh and a shake of her head.

"Then he wasn't man enough for you."

Pink blooms across her cheeks, and it brings a scattering of freckles into sharp relief. I wonder about the freckles hidden from view. "Hmmm. Devastatingly handsome *and* sweet. That's a dangerous combination Mr. Whiskey." She walks her fingers up my lapel. And just like that — the arousal I've valiantly held at bay comes flooding back.

"I'm not sweet," I protest.

This time, her laugh is low and sultry. And it goes straight to my balls. "I bet…" She runs her palm across my chest. "That underneath that tough guy exterior, you're nothing but a big, squishy teddy bear."

"Nope," I scoff, flexing under her touch. "Bad to the bone."

Her eyes flare with a hungry light. "Prove it," she challenges. "Make good on your promise to make me moan."

Jesus.

My cock leaps to attention. This isn't the first time a woman's come on to me, but it *is* the first time I'm so turned on I feel drunk. The volume has tripled in Kirkwood Hall, and with it comes the smell of money and power. I'll be pocketing a portion of that later this evening, but in the meantime, why not take a walk on the wild side? The band has started to play, and if I'm going to disappear, now's the time. But… condoms. *Fucking hell.* "I didn't pack condoms."

"I have them."

Of course she does. "Do you want to take a picture of me and text it to someone?"

Her mouth twitches. "I can handle you."

"What makes you so sure?"

"For starters, there are security cameras everywhere. For seconds, I can handle myself. And for thirds —" laughter flickers through her eyes, "You're a big teddy bear and I'd bet the house that you wouldn't hurt me unless I begged you to."

A laugh rumbles deep in my belly. She's not wrong — at least about the hurting. I'm no fucking teddy bear. "You're crazy." And sexy as fuck. My hands itch to learn her curves, the little divots and mounds. Where she's soft and where her skin molds to her bones.

"Entirely possible," she agrees, pursing her lips. "Aren't we all a little crazy?"

She has a point.

"And isn't it about exploring whether or not our particular brand of crazy lines up?" she presses, drawing her fingers along the inside of my tuxedo jacket.

Energy ripples down my spine. I've never heard it expressed in those terms, but yeah. I've never met a woman whose appetite matched my own, who accepted the darkness inside of me without trying to reform me. I stare into her eyes, and for a second that stretches into eternity, I feel like I'm at the edge of a chasm. Like whatever I choose in my next breath will define me. There will be no going back from this moment.

We speak at the same time. "I know a room."

Chapter Three

I place my hand at the small of her back and steer her out of Kirkwood, through the sculpture hall and down around Atkins Auditorium. The sounds of the gala fade until there's nothing but the echoes of our footsteps in the empty hall.

"How did you—"

"Not my first gala."

"Not your first hook-up," she corrects with a laugh.

I push open the door to the family bathroom, and usher her in, spinning and pinning her to the door while I turn the lock on the handle. "You sure about this?"

She answers by wrapping a hand around my neck and pulling. Our mouths unite in a violent crash of teeth and tongues. Lips alternately soft, then demanding. She's set off a chain reaction within me that will only end in an explosion of epic proportions. She works the buttons of my shirt, while I shrug out of my jacket. It's sweet relief when her fingers trace the Celtic dragon tattoo over my heart, then slide down my abdomen to pause at the scar left from a knife fight when I was sixteen.

Before she can release the buttons on my slacks, I take her wrists and draw her arms over her head. I like her this way, lipstick smudged, hair mussed, eyes wild, tits out, thanks to the arch in her back. "Just so you know," I rasp. "I will do whatever you ask. However you want it. You're calling the shots. Clear?"

She nods, biting back a grin. "And what if I want it just the way you described it? Coming on your tongue? Fucking me from behind?"

"Whatever you want."

"I want it all."

I press my body against hers, still holding her wrists above us, and take her mouth. Slowly this time, so I can taste every part of her, memorize the velvet of her tongue sliding against mine. I become drunk on her, my brain spinning as our kissing intensifies. She rocks her hips into me, grinding against my erection, and making a guttural noise in the back of her throat. With an answering groan, I pull myself away and trail kisses down her neck, nipping the tendon at the hollow of her throat.

"I should warn you," she says breathlessly. "Kissing my neck makes me all kinds of crazy."

I respond by licking a path up to the dip behind her jaw. "If I touched you, would you be wet?" I whisper into her ear.

She answers with a low laugh. "What do you think?"

"I wanna hear you say it."

"That my panties are soaked? That my thighs are slick from wanting you?"

Fuuuuuuuuuuck.

I can't recall ever being this aroused, this hungry, this close to losing my shit and giving over to purely animal instincts. I kiss her again, hard, and I swear I can feel the heat of her pussy through all the layers of fabric that separate us. I release her wrists and drop to my knees, wrapping a hand around her ankle. The tail of her snake begins about three fingers above her ankle bone, and on close examination, I let out a low whistle of appreciation. "Beautiful," I murmur, lifting her leg and placing a kiss on the blue, gold, and green ink. The tattooing is a work of art — the scales so intricate as to seem real, especially when she flexes her muscles. Her leg trembles beneath my hand, twitching when I kiss a particularly sensitive spot. She eggs me on with tiny moans and gasps, and words like "More," and "Yes, that."

I shift my position when I reach her knee, drawing my fingers around the back of her thigh and up, stopping when I brush against lace. "What's this?" I tease, slipping my finger under the elastic, and tracing underneath until I hit... warm metal. I freeze. "Whattheeverloving*fuck?*" I rasp. The lace is a goddamned holster and she's packing.

"I said I could take care of myself," she says with a nervous laugh.

"Is it loaded?" I give myself a shake. "Of course it's loaded." I glance up at her. "Seriously? You're packing at a fundraiser gala?"

"I pack everywhere," she snaps. "If that bothers you..." Her voice trails off and she begins to shift away.

"Hold on, I didn't say it bothers me. It was just a... surprise. That's all. I have no problem with you carrying." Unless of course, she walked into my club. My security detail packs in plain sight — mostly to send a message to some of the more... ethically challenged members. No guns inside my club. Ever. I've banned members in the past for violating that code, and I won't hesitate to do so again. But she'll never know that. We might be having fun right now, but it ends the second she pushes through that door. "Don't worry," I say, giving her a wicked grin. "I love the taste of danger." I caress the inside of her other leg, the one that's bare up to her panties. And sure enough, she's soaked. I graze the fabric with a knuckle sliding across her swollen folds.

It's hot as fuck, seeing how aroused she is. I wrap a finger around the thin lace strap and give a jerk. It snaps free. I make short work of the other side, and what remains of her lacy thong slides to the floor. She kicks them out of the way with a laugh. "I didn't want those anyway."

"Open your legs," I say gruffly, as I push her dress out of the way.

She widens her stance, and I press a kiss to the inside of her thigh, taking my time as I kiss and lick, and suck my way toward heaven. The scent of her arousal thickens my blood. My balls are heavy and hard. I rise, bracing a hand on the wall next to her hip, and as I make my way to her pussy, I take my first taste of her at the spot where her thighs touch. She's sweet and musky, and I'm reminded of the ocean breeze in spring. I groan with the delight of it as I lick her thighs clean. I'm addicted, and all it took was one taste. How have I lived this long without her flavor? I'm clearly not thinking straight, but ask me if I give a flying fuck. Not with pussy this sweet begging for my mouth. I flick my tongue along the outside of her folds and she spreads her legs wider, hand dropping to my head. "Bring it, hot stuff," she says.

I can tell she's smiling. A glance up confirms it, and our eyes lock. Holding her gaze, I slide a finger through her slick seam, lightly back and forth then circling her clit until her eyes glaze and her tongue slips out to wet her lips. Her hips slowly rock, as if she's holding back, trying to hold still.

"Don't hold back. I wanna see you let go."

She gives me a crooked smile. "Don't worry, you will."

I nip the inside of her thigh, then slowly lick through her folds. The taste of her floods my mouth and the buzz is better than my finest whiskey. I lick again with the flat of my tongue, and circle her clit, lapping at the tight point until she cries out. "I'm going to come in like two seconds if you keep doing that."

I laugh low in my throat and draw her clit into my mouth, sucking as I cover the bundle of nerves with my tongue. Sure enough, a shudder rips through her and her legs squeeze my head as her fingers pull hard on my hair. But I'm a relentless motherfucker, and I don't stop. I've barely started. I thrust my tongue into her tight, wet channel and fuck her like I will with my cock while pressing a thumb to her sensitized clit. I start with slow thrusts, then change up my rhythm, and just at the point I think she's going to come again, I pull out and bite the inside of her thigh.

This earns me a violent hair yank. "Don't *do* that," she grits through clenched teeth. "*Don't. Stop.*"

"What's the magic word?" I tease.

"I will hurt you if you stop."

I can't help the laugh that erupts from my belly. "Is your cunt hungry for more?"

She growls, thrusting her hips, seeking relief. I'm not an asshole, I'm going to give it to her, just like I promised, but I love seeing her on the verge of coming undone. It pulls at something deep in my chest — like a puzzle piece sliding home.

I slide a finger inside her, then two, scissoring, then curling toward the spot I know will drive her wild. Again, I return my mouth to her clit — worshipping it like the treasure it is. This time she breaks apart with a cry, body freezing then shuddering over and over again, breath coming in harsh gasps as she flies, then slowly returns to earth. "You're beautiful," I utter, overcome by the vision of her. It's not a platitude. If I never see her again, I will remember her like this for the rest of my life. Cheeks pink, head back, exposing the slender column of her throat as her body trembles *because of me*.

She grins down at me. "I think you promised me a fuck."

"You're insatiable," I say with a laugh, shaking my head. Because, seriously? I've never been with a woman who could match my appetite. I love it. Except for the tiny voice of warning that cautions me to run. Because it's a woman like this — a woman I've only dreamed about — who could break me. I push that thought as far out of my head as I can, and rise, hand on my belt. "Condoms?"

With a sly grin, she slips her hand underneath the vee of her neckline and reaches between her breasts, pulling out a condom like it's a fucking dollar bill. I can't help but laugh. "You're kidding."

She flicks her eyebrows. "A girl scout is always prepared."

A vision of her in a miniskirt and green sash flits in front of my eyes. Hot. As. Fuck. "Dress. Off," I growl.

All it earns me is a saucy smile. She throws my words back at me. "What's the magic word?"

I cage her in. "A mind-blowing orgasm."

She bites her lip, corner of her mouth curling up, then pulls up her dress. I step back to give her room, and help her pull the stretchy fabric over her head. I forget to breathe when I lay eyes on the see-through blush fabric of her strapless bra, flesh spilling out over the top. She unhooks the bra and it falls to the floor between us. I bite back a groan. Her breasts are full and lush, nipples erect and dark. A color that reminds me of sun-kissed peaches. I bend to take a nipple into my mouth, hand coming to her other breast to caress her silky curve. I could lose myself in breasts like these, in their pillowy softness. I regret we're not in bed where she could ride me, and I could lose myself in the soft sway of them.

As quickly as I can muster, with a mouthful of luscious titty, I toe off my shoes, grateful I wore slip-ons, then drop my pants. She pushes my shoulders. "I want to see."

I take a step back, kicking my pants and boxer briefs across the floor. My cock juts out, hard and long.

She steps forward to trace a finger along my length. Her touch is like an electric shock. I shudder, cock jerking. Again, regret teases at the edge of my consciousness, whispering *if only*. But there aren't *if onlies* for men like me — only giving and taking in the moment. That's all I get, and I mean to give and take all I can from this moment. "Turn around," I say roughly. "Hands on the wall."

She complies, shooting a wicked glance over her shoulder as she spreads her legs and tips her ass high, so that I have a full view of her swollen pussy. I commit this moment to memory as I step forward and run my palm down her spine, then across her ass cheeks before sliding my hand between her legs to cup her sex.

"Is that condom on yet?" Her voice is tight with impatience. I squeeze her pussy, then withdraw my hand to sheath myself. I step behind her, caressing her hips, and teasing my cock at her entrance. I bend and bite her neck where it meets her shoulder. "Patience, grasshopper."

She replies with a grunt and a roll of her hips back toward my cock.

"Is this what you want?" I say with a grunt as I squeeze her hips and slam my cock into her, balls deep."

"Yesssss," she hisses. "More." She wriggles her hips, pressing her ass back and squeezing my cock. Her channel is tight, and so, so hot. My eyes roll back, because, Jeezus, this is good. Maybe the best ever.

I wrap an arm around her hips, settling my fingers at her clit, while my other hand comes to her breast, seeking and finding a nipple. I pinch.

"That, too," she grunts, arching her back.

I begin to move, long slow strokes.

"Harder," she begs. "Just like you promised." Her words come out in breathless pants.

I thrust harder, slamming into her, then slowly pulling back out, almost all the way, then pushing back into the deepest part of her. She lets out a low moan, and I tap dance my fingers over her clit. Energy flies through my body, spooling up my legs, and circling low in my groin. Words stop, and my focus narrows to a sharp point — skin slapping, breath gasping, moans and broken words punctuating the silence like starbursts. She comes first, squeezing and rippling around me with a cry. My vision spots as I let go. My head explodes, and I swallow the roar I'm dying to let out by biting my lip to the point I taste blood.

I pull her close, not quite ready for the moment to end. But... condoms. I clasp the end and pull out, quickly disposing of it in the trash. When I glance her direction, she's flipped around and is leaning against the door with an amused smile. "I'll never think of this place the same way."

I flash her a grin. "Neither will I." Regret presses against my chest. I don't want this to be the end. It was too good, and instinctively, I know it would get better with practice. I gently wipe her with the tissues I've grabbed. I can't stop the words that spill out next. "We could ditch this party and I could properly bed you."

Her eyes warm. She wants it, too. "I'm sorry... I can't." There's regret in her voice, and that soothes my mildly bruised ego. I'm not used to being turned down. Ever. "But if by chance our paths cross again…" Her voice drifts off, but the implication is clear.

"You're something else, Roxi."

She beams. "So are you, Mr. Whiskey. So are you."

I bend to retrieve her bra and dress, then turn, offering her privacy while I put myself back together. Her hand lands on my arm, and I turn. Somehow, she manages to look flawless, not freshly fucked. "How do you do that?" I murmur.

"Do what?"

"Manage to look perfect?"

Her mouth quirks. "It's my superpower." Her eyes soften, and she cups my cheek. "Thank you for this."

"The pleasure was all mine." Understatement of the year. "Believe me," I add wryly. "You slip out first, I'll follow in a few minutes."

She presses a kiss to my cheek, and a twinge arrows straight to my heart. "I'll never forget you, Danny," she whispers as she steps to the door.

"Wait," I call before she turns the handle.

She glances back.

"At least tell me your last name."

Her sly smile returns. "It's Rickoli. Roxi Rickoli."

"Nice meeting you, Roxi Rickoli," I say, wanting to say so much more but knowing I can't.

She turns the handle and slips out without a backward glance.

Fuck. Me.

Chapter Four

I wait three minutes before slipping out the door and heading back to the gala. Harrison pounces on me as soon as I re-enter Kirkwood Hall. "Where've you been, man? We've been looking all over for you."

"Taking care of business," I deadpan. "Do we have a table?"

"Stockton's out tonight. But I'll be there, and so will Templeton."

"Who else?"

"Ferrari's in."

My gut clenches. "I didn't know he was in town?" Vincent Ferrari is a dirty, slippery sonofabitch. I'm pretty sure his real-estate company is a shell organization. But he pays his dues on time, and as far as I'm concerned, his money is as good as anyone else's — even if I think he's a bigger asshole than me — which is saying something.

Harrison's lip curls in disgust. "He's over at the poker table. Honestly, I don't understand why you don't give him the boot."

"You should know the answer to that," I growl. Money

is power. Information is more power. Business and emotions don't mix. All lessons I learned too young. Harrison has no clue about the people I'm responsible for, and that alone keeps me hustling. Tom Pendergast saved Kansas City from the Great Depression. His grandson is doing hard time for a laundry list of crimes. Money and influence are as fleeting as the spring storms that pile up to the west every season, unless you were lucky enough to be born into a billion-dollar fortune like Harrison and his cohorts. I might be as wealthy as they are now, but they'll never understand what it's like to wonder where your next meal is coming from. So, it doesn't matter what I think of Ferrari — only that I help him part with a fraction of his fortune.

Harrison stares at me for a long second, then shakes his head. "Your business, man."

"Which has benefitted you greatly," I point out. He knows it too. He secured sixty-percent of his startup funding for Steele Conglomerate from deals he made at the Whiskey Den.

He nods grimly. "I know, I know. It's just…"

"Just what?"

"Don't you want more?"

I scoff. "Do you?"

"More than my business?" His face pulls tight for a fleeting second. "Yeah. Yeah, I guess I do." There's surprise in his voice, as if he's just discovered this.

"Jesus. Whoever she is, she must have your cock in irons."

Harrison snorts. "You don't know the half of it."

"Tell me about it over a whiskey after the game. Who else is in?"

"Dmitri, and some mutual friend of his and Vince's. Ivo Rostyak?"

"Number Thirty-Five." I see him about once a year and I like him about as much as I like Dmitri and Vince. I'm pretty sure Ivo is Russian mob. He flies in about every six months from New York, and meets with Vince or Dmitri, sometimes both. Never brought a guest, not very talkative. He's sat in on games when he's been in town. "Pays his dues on time." Tonight's game feels very East meets West, although Vince is based in Chicago, and I see him monthly. I'd like to see him less. "Any lady companions?"

Harrison shakes his head.

"I'll let Lisa know." I pull out my phone and begin typing.

"Has she given you any indication who knocked her up?" Harrison growls, hand curling into a fist.

"Calm down, I have first dibs on the asshole. And no, wild horses won't drag it from her."

"I'd like to help out when the baby's born."

"What — are you offering to babysit? I've already told her that her expenses are covered, and she can take as much post-baby time as she needs before she comes back." I recognize we may be talking years, but I take care of my own, and Lisa's been my right hand from the get-go. I still haven't figured out what I'm going to do once the baby comes. But I'll work it out. I always do.

Harrison snorts. "I'm not volunteering to change diapers, but I'd hire help for her."

And this, in a nutshell, is why Harrison and I remain friends. He takes care of his own, too. And he knows how valuable Lisa is to the Whiskey Den. I clap him on the shoulder. "I appreciate the offer, and I'll keep it in mind."

Harrison scans the crowd. "Isn't that your redhead dancing over there?"

I look to where he points, and fight the stab of jealousy

that slices through me. She's dancing with someone who looks to be as old as her grandfather. I don't like that his hand drifts perilously close to her ass. Her naked as fuck ass. But we agreed. Just sex. A knot presses against my sternum. For a split second, I wish my life was other than it was — that I wasn't emotionally stunted, that I didn't carry the name Pendergast, that at the end of the day I'd get the girl. But that's not my life, and I've accepted that. Mostly.

I take my leave from the gala after promising Muffy a significant donation. Earlier than I'd intended, but this night has been nothing like I expected, and I want an hour to myself before I have to put my poker face on. I pull into my spot in the West Bottoms, within sight of the Whiskey Den door, pleased to see my favorite bouncer, Oscar, manning the door tonight. The West Bottoms is a neighborhood still in transition, but my great-grandfather got his start just a few blocks from here, working at his brother's bar. Locating the Whiskey Den here seemed fitting, like I could rewrite history somehow.

It's quiet in the Den. I wave to a couple of members holed up in the leather wingbacks in the corner, and slip behind the bar to pour myself a drink. "I didn't expect you for another hour." Lisa, my bar manager gives me a healthy dose of side-eye. "Everything okay?"

I shrug. "Sure. I just needed to clear my head before the game tonight." Because I can't get a certain redhead out of it.

"Who's coming tonight?"

I tell her, then take my drink to the office, my private sanctuary. I do my best thinking in the small room I've decorated in dark paneling, leather wingbacks, and an enormous oak desk that belonged to grandpa Tom — the only physical connection I have to my family legacy. It's clear but for my laptop, folded shut in front of a high-end swivel chair. In my mind's eye, I can see Roxi spread across it, head released back, wearing nothing but stilettos and that lacy thigh holster. Just like that, I'm hard again. I regret not pressing for her number. If I shut my eyes, I can still taste her. But it's best Roxi Rickoli stays nothing but a sexy memory, albeit one I'll be revisiting for a long time to come.

Lisa buzzes me when the first of the players arrive, and I make my way to the back room, taking my seat at the far end of the circular table, directly across from the door. Behind me is a bookcase that holds among other things, a box of Cuban cigars, two boxes of poker chips, and multiple sets of unused cards. The men filter in one by one, drinks in hand. Ferrari takes a seat to my left. Harrison pulls out a chair next to him, a move that surprises me, given his dislike for Vince. Dmitri takes the seat to my right, Robert Templeton chooses the seat next to Harrison. Ivo is the last to enter and takes the remaining seat.

I spread my arms. "Welcome gentlemen. To recap, the buy-in for each round is fifty-thousand. The house keeps thirty-percent of the buy-in. We'll take a break between each round for you to make your payments." I hold out my hand. "Phones?"

With a nod of agreement, each man drops his phone into my hand. I place them on the bookcase behind me, then pull out the box of chips. Once they've been passed around, I sit. I make a show of unwrapping the brand-new deck of cards and spreading them across the table for the players to see, Vegas style. When no one objects, I sweep the cards up and begin to shuffle. The group is quiet tonight, no doubt because of Ivo's permanent scowl, and Vince's posturing. I don't like the way Vince is staring at Ivo — with something akin to avarice, and I especially don't like the way Ivo's eyes are shifting around. Something is definitely up between those two, and I'll be watching like a hawk tonight. I deal two cards face down, and the next card face up. Robert has the highest card on the table and opens the bidding. An eerie silence settles over the table that I don't like. Energy is crackling between Vince, Dmitri and Ivo, and it's impacting the play. Harrison bows out after I deal the fourth card. Robert drops out after the fifth. I deal the sixth card. Dmitri is showing a pair of sevens, Vince, a queen, and Ivo the beginnings of a Jack high straight. Vince raises the ante, and the other two follow.

"All in?" I ask before I deal the final card face-down. They nod. I deal. Ivo drops his cards in disgust when Vince shows three queens, then rakes up the pile of chips. Harrison wins the second round, as Ivo becomes more agitated. I stare at him hard. He rakes a hand through his hair, and it's soaked at his temple. "Need a break Ivo?"

He aims a glance at Vince that looks almost frightened, then he shakes his head. Does he owe Vince? Rumor has it that Vince has been known to 'lend a hand', and then collect brutally if the lendee came up short at the agreed upon time. Now I wonder if the rumors have merit. I call for the ante. Ivo pulls at his collar, but pushes in his chips.

Dmitri folds when the betting opens. Harrison and Robert drop out after the fourth card. After the fifth, I expect Ivo to fold. He's showing junk — a two of clubs, a four of hearts and a six of spades. Instead, he doubles down. "Are you sure?" I ask, incredulous.

Ivo glares at me and nods once, hand fisting on the table.

"You've got three of a kind at best. Vince is working on a flush." I don't like to see people waste their money. I look to Vince, who looks like a cat in front of a bowl of cream. "I don't know what's going on between you two, but this is it for tonight."

"*No.*" Ivo rasps, eyes widening like a caged animal. "One more round."

I shake my head, mouth drawing into a thin line. This isn't the first time I've seen the clutch of gambling addiction choke a player. "One more round isn't enough to cover your losses," I point out. "Give it up. Play another day."

He shakes his head staring at Vince. "I'll be good for it. You know I will."

Vince's expression is hard. Implacable. Every muscle in his body is tense, poised to spring. I make the call because I'll be damned if this devolves into a fist-fight.

"No. *Please,*" Ivo begs. "I'll give you Ana. She's yours."

Vince's eyes light hungrily as I leap out of my chair and drag Ivo to his feet. "Like hell you will," I shout, seeing red. "We don't deal in humans. *Ever.*" I shake him hard enough to make his teeth rattle. "Do. You. Understand?" Behind me, chairs scrape as everyone stands. "You're out. Banned. You're lucky I don't beat you to a pulp," I say as I push him around the table and out the door. "Oscar," I yell, tightening my grip on Ivo. I dimly register the main room has gone silent. Oscar meets me in front of the bar, and I shove Ivo at him. "Throw him out. He's banned. See to it he never comes back."

"I can explain—" Ivo stutters.

I cut him off. "I don't give a shit. There are no do overs. *Ever*. Take care of him Oscar." I spin on my heel and stalk back to the poker room. "I'll cover Ivo's losses."

Harrison speaks first. "No worries, man. It's not your fault he's a douchebag."

"I want my money," Vince states flatly.

Of course he does. Disgust rises up, burning the back of my throat. "Give me five minutes." I leave the room again and walk down the hall past the stock room, to my office. Once inside, I initiate a Venmo transfer to Vince. It's the right thing to do, but Harrison letting it go was also the right thing to do. Vince doesn't need the money. This is about ego. I grind my molars, waiting for the transfer to go through. From here on out, I'm applying a new layer of vetting to my members. No assholes or douchebags.

Chapter Five

I oversleep. I never oversleep. Worse? I never even made it to bed. A glance at the coffee table shows a half-full tumbler of whiskey, now watered down with last night's ice. Next to me, my laptop screen is dark. The last thing I remember was putting it aside to shut my eyes while I waited for a database return. But it doesn't matter. This one, like all the other searches I've made in the last two weeks, came up empty.

I stretch, working out a kink in my neck, and glance at my watch. If I hustle, I can still make my eight a.m. training session with Mariah Sanchez, the personal trainer and coxswain Harrison and his crew buddies have hired for their boat. She might barely top five-feet, but the woman is a beast. And even though I refuse on a daily basis to take up rowing again, I've at least agreed to train with the team. Mostly for the entertainment value of seeing Mariah boss the titans of tech around like a Marine sergeant. I've never seen giant men whimper like they do when she gives them the evil eye and tells them to multiple sets of burpees, mountain climbers, and one-armed pushups.

Today, that evil-eye is trained on me when I walk in at eight-oh-five. "You're late."

"I know. I'm sorry. Rough night."

"Nothing a little sweat won't cure."

Or a lot. Buckets full. I bite back a groan when she tells me to warm up with a three-mile jog. "Meet me back here in fifteen."

"That's not a jog, that's a goddamned sprint."

"You have a problem with that?"

Fuck yes, I do. I'm exhausted, pissed-off, and the worst case of blue balls. But I'm not a whiner. I glare back. "See you in fifteen."

"If you hurry you can catch the rest of the team."

My mind whirls as I rush to catch up to Harrison, Stockton and their team. Mariah is exactly the kind of no-nonsense person I should hire to work my bar when Lisa goes on maternity leave in a few months. Even though my legs protest, I manage to catch the guys. "Hey," I say by way of greeting.

Harrison raises a hand, and I match my pace to his. "So I'm going to need to hire someone when Lisa has her baby. Think Mariah'd be interested?"

"No," he growls. "Absolutely not."

"She'd be perfect. Didn't you say she has catering experience?"

"I said no." Harrison shoots a glare my way before turning his eyes back to the road.

"Why the fuck not?" I ask, exasperation and exhaustion getting the better of me. "I need someone I can trust. Someone who won't take any shit."

"Ask that red headed lady then."

"Roxi?" I nearly stumble to a stop. "I've been looking

for her for two weeks. She's a goddamned ghost. I've run searches for her, made inquiries, and keep coming up empty handed." I hate to admit it, especially to someone like Harrison, but I think I got played. Even though the sex was fanfuckingtastic.

"Then find someone else. Sparky's off limits."

"Jeezus. What crawled up your ass and laid eggs?" I snipe.

"Nothing," he snaps back.

"Sounds like you're overdue for a fucking," I taunt.

He makes a strangled sound and shakes his head. Then it hits me. He hasn't been getting laid. Steele fucks more women than anyone I've ever met, and for him to have dried up… well, let's just say I no longer give a shit about making it back to the gym in fifteen minutes, because this development is hilarious. I stop, and bend, the laughter making my sides hurt. Harrison jogs a few more paces and stops too. "It's not that funny."

"Oh yes, it is," I say once my laughter has subsided. "Who is she?"

"Doesn't matter."

"Oh yes it does. This is the same chick that ditched you, isn't it? And now your blue balls are worse than mine."

"Shut. Up."

"I'm gonna find out, you know. I always find shit out."

"Like you've found Roxi?"

That's a low blow and he knows it. But it shuts me up, and my dark mood returns. "Let's go. I don't want extra pushups."

"Too late for that. You screwed our pace."

"Fuck off."

"I'd love to," Harrison's wry answer comes from behind me, as I push myself trying to catch the pack. If I can't get laid, I might as well be sore all over. At least it will take my mind off my aching balls. Mariah works all of us extra hard today. Apparently I'm not the only one in a foul mood. By the time I pull into the parking lot it's after ten-thirty. I greet Oscar and tell him I'm not to be disturbed until after noon today. And no clients inside until one, because I need to count stock. Lisa's too pregnant to be standing on ladders taking inventory, so I've agreed to take over keeping the bar stocked until she comes back from maternity leave.

I trail a hand along the vintage mahogany bar that lines one side of my place. There's a vibe that never ceases to calm me — even on my worst days. An escape from the troubles and pressures of the outside world. Here is a haven where the whiskey is magic, and the leather chairs embrace you like a pair of loving arms.

"Lisa?" I call as I head for the stock room. "I swear if you're on a ladder…"

My smile dies as I round the corner. Someone's precariously perched on the top of the stepladder — just like the manual warns you *not* to do — and it's definitely not Lisa. No, I recognize those long legs and lush curves, and the long red hair that accompanies them. "Roxi?" I say, incredulous.

She squeaks and turns, losing her purchase. I rush to break her fall, trying my best to catch her and the bottle of whiskey she's holding. We tumble to the floor with a crash. I brace for the sound of breaking glass, but none comes. She's stretched out on top of me, and I run my hand down her spine, mentally checking for broken bones. "Are you okay? Did the bottle break?" Frustration at the lack of anything I've found on her returns, and with equal force, so does my arousal. I cover it by yelling, because Christ, her tits are pressing into my chest. "What in the hell are you doing here?"

She squirms, and my erection throbs between us, hot and hard. "Is that how you greet all the ladies?" She asks with a coy smile.

I'm flustered, and bothered, and not thinking with my right mind. "Are you packing?"

Her smile widens. "Are you going to frisk me?"

"I'm going to do a helluva lot more than frisk you," I growl as I roll us to the side, and rise, bringing her with me. I turn her around and propel her into the hall, steering her toward my office.

"Ooh," she says casting an eager glance over her shoulder. "Are you going to strip search me?"

A giggle escapes her, and it gives me pause. She's got to be teasing me, egging me on to see what I'm going to do. "Do I need to?"

"Hmm, that depends."

I shut the door behind me and lock it. If she's packing, she's wearing a leg holster. I didn't feel a harness across her back when I was checking for injury. "Ass on the desk. Now."

She complies, eyes expectant. Warning bells are screaming in my head. The more I try to intimidate her, the more excited she becomes, and I'm discovering it arouses the fuck out of me, this one-upmanship.

"Lie back on your elbows, spread your legs. She's grinning like a goddamned Cheshire Cat, and it sets something on fire, deep inside my belly. I loom over her, sliding my fingers along the underside of the white vee-neck tee shirt she's wearing. "First, I'm going to frisk you. Slowly."

I take my time, caressing each curve, sliding under the swell of her breast, avoiding the most sensitive part of her there, because I won't give her the satisfaction. Yet. By the time my hand is at the waistband of her black slacks, her breathing is shallow. I caress the curve of a hip, then across the gentle swell of her belly to the other. Her hips rock up to meet my hand, but I avoid her pussy, avoid giving her the friction I can see she wants. Her mouth has dropped open, and she's watching me through heavy lidded eyes. It's easy to see she's not wearing a thigh holster, but I caress the inside of her thighs anyway. I find the holster at her left ankle. I draw up the pant leg and begin to work the holster free.

This is the first time I see worry in her eyes. "Don't worry. I'm not going to hurt you. Unless you want me to," I add with a wink. "But I have a strict 'no guns' rule in my establishment. I remove the gun from its holster and double check the safety. I half expect a Glock, because the thought has crossed my mind that maybe she's a Fed, but it's smaller than the standard issue government weapon. At any rate, I tuck the weapon into my desk drawer. "I'll return this to you when you leave. But in the meantime." I bend over her again, running my hand down her thigh. "Unless you have objections, I believe a strip search is in order."

She hesitates, and I freeze, hand at her knee.

"Roxi?" Her hesitation makes me uneasy, and I step away. "Why are you here?"

"Because I missed you," she answers with a slow smile. Whatever internal struggle was taking place inside her mind has been resolved, because her hand moves to the button on her slacks. "I'm ready for my strip search now."

She says it so primly that I burst out laughing. "God I missed your humor," I say as my hand joins hers and I help her shimmy out of her pants.

"See?" She drops her knees wide. "No weapons."

"I'm not so sure. You'll need to remove your shirt."

"And if I refuse?"

"Then I'll have to turn you over and spank you."

Her eyes light. "Promise?"

I nod slowly. I'd love nothing more than to see my palm print pink up that sweet porcelain ass.

Her voice drops as a blush spreads across her cheeks. "Would you do it anyway?"

"If you asked nicely." Because, hell, yes.

She pulls her shirt over her head, drops it to the floor alongside her pants, and flips to her side, propping up her head with her hand. She's wearing a matching see-through set of barely blush pink underwear. So transparent, I can see her neatly trimmed copper curls as easily as I can see her dusky areolas, and the burgeoning peaks of her nipples. My mind is stuck on a treadmill. She came here today to get laid. *Obviously*. But why? And how did she find me? And why haven't I been able to find her? The more primal part of my brain shouts back who cares? Just the other day I was fantasizing about this very thing — Roxi naked on my desk. *And she's here*. Who the fuck cares why? Take the pussy, ask questions later.

"Danny?" she asks, voice soft and breathy.

Whatever it is, no matter how insane, I already know I'll say yes. Her amber eyes are wide, her mouth pouty, and her voice… might just bring me to my knees. "What is it sweetheart?" I reply softly.

"Would you spank me?"

Jesus fuck. I swear my cock grows to epic proportions, that I've never been this hard, ever. I nod, because I've momentarily lost the capacity to speak. "On your hands and knees," I say when I can speak again. I don't recognize my voice.

Her panties are cut high across her ass, leaving the sweet curves of her cheeks exposed. The slap echoes when it lands, and a pink mark springs up. My next strike is on the other side, because symmetry. "Is that how you like it?"

She nods, wiggling her ass. "Yes, just like that."

I continue, mesmerized by the color that splashes across her flesh, and the way she begins to rock her hips, like she's seeking friction after each blow. "Does this make you wet?"

"God, yes," she says with a little moan.

"Show me," I rasp. "Touch yourself and show me."

She slips a hand underneath her panties, and I slap her as she fingers herself, which draws an even deeper moan from her throat. I can tell if I continue, she'll come in short order, but I want her to come on my fingers, or my mouth, or on my cock.

"Show me," I order.

She pulls her hand from her panties and holds it out, fingers glistening with her wetness. I lick them clean, the taste of her even better than I remembered.

I'm overcome with the need to be inside her, to encase myself in her tight heat. I jerk open a drawer, grab a condom, and toss it onto the desk as I start to pull my shirt free. Roxi watches avidly as I release the buttons on my shirt, making pleased little humming sounds as more of my chest is exposed. She spins and scrambles off the desk, crowding into me, forcing me into my giant leather swivel chair. She drops to her knees, raking her fingernails over my abs before fiddling with the buttons on my slacks. The sound of the zipper fills the space, and it's erotic as fuck. Even more so when she slips a hand underneath the waistband of my boxer briefs and releases my cock. I let out a noise of pure animal pleasure as she grips my length and pulls up, squeezing just underneath the crown.

She bends, hair spilling across my lap like a blanket, my hips jerk when her tongue skates across the head, lapping up the sheen of precome that has gathered. It's hot, and wet, and when she takes me fully into her mouth, tongue sliding against my shaft, I think I must have died. All rational thought flies from my head, there's only her mouth on my cock, sucking and licking at me until I think I'm going to explode. "Stop," I utter through clenched teeth. "Condom."

She raises her head, eyes wide, lips wet, and gives me an assessing stare.

"*Now*, Roxi."

She laughs quietly, then proceeds to take her damn time rising and perches on the edge of the desk, hand hovering at the waistband of her panties, mouth twitching. She's fucking taunting me and loving every second.

"Roxi." My voice is heavy with warning.

She smirks. "Oooh, are you going to spank me some more?"

I honestly don't know what I'm going to do, or if I'm going to survive the exquisite agony of waiting. "Panties off, condom on," I growl.

She hooks a thumb underneath the fabric, like she's going to pull, but then changes her mind, and her hands reach for her bra clasp. I can see the second the clasp is free, the front gaps slightly, and she shimmies her shoulders, freeing the straps, and dropping the bra. I'm a fan of the striptease, the way it builds anticipation. I lick my lips, imagining what it will be like when I take a tight bud into my mouth. She turns around, and bares her ass to me first.

"Tease," I utter, gripping the arms of the chair.

"Yes, indeed." I can hear the smile in her voice.

"Just remember, payback, sweetheart."

"I'm looking forward to it," she shoots back as she slowly turns, kicking her panties off. The copper curls at her apex are wet with her arousal, and I want so badly to touch her. But I want her pussy on my cock more.

"Come here."

She swipes the condom off the desk and tears it open. But she's not done torturing me. She runs a finger down my shaft, so hard it's dark red, tracing the vein that throbs painfully. "So big," she whispers. "So hungry."

"I swear to god, Roxi," I choke. "Give me the condom."

She makes a humming noise in her throat. "Good things come to those who wait."

"I'm done waiting," I say tightly.

It's sweet relief when she rolls the condom over my aching cock, then climbs on the chair, positioning herself above me. "This is the best part," she murmurs, sliding onto me, seating herself fully. At this moment, I agree, because fuck, I want to weep with the relief of finally being wrapped in her. She wiggles her hips, and her walls squeeze tight around me. We're not exactly at an angle for thrusting, but she begins to rock, taking a slow languid pace at odds with our breathing, which is rapid and shallow. She offers up her tits. "Suck."

Like I'd ever say no. I dive in, taking one peak and sucking hard, grazing my teeth along the sensitive skin, while I roll her other nipple between my thumb and forefinger, giving a little pinch. She grunts in satisfaction, and clenches harder around my cock as she continues to rock.

"I've dreamed of this, of you filling me up," she utters on a sharp exhale. "I'm close," she pants.

Her movements become more rhythmic, more intense, and I follow her, sucking and licking like a starving man, meeting her rocking hips with pulses of my own, pushing into her as far as I can. She bears down at the same time as she cries out, and I'm right there with her, orgasm exploding out of me with the force of an atom bomb. I grip her hips hard enough to bruise as I empty myself into her with a shout, vision spotting and going black. She drops her head to my shoulder, breathing hard. "Fuck, Roxi. What was that?" I ask when I can finally speak again.

"I have no idea." Her voice is filled with surprise, wonder, even. "But I liked it."

Understatement of the year. "Yeah. Me too."

We sit quietly, wrapped in each other, lost in a post-orgasmic fog. I realize two things as my brain boots back to life. First, I'm utterly and completely addicted to sex with this woman, and I will do anything to keep her close. Second, and more sobering, is that I need to stay as far away from Roxi Rickoli as I can. Because she's exactly the type of woman who will be my downfall.

Chapter Six

_____

*S*he slips off my lap and we begin the ritual of putting ourselves back together. It shouldn't surprise me, but it does, that there's no awkwardness, or pretense. As if getting a little kinky and fucking in my office was the most normal thing in the world.

I watch fascinated, as she dresses. Roxi is completely at ease with her body, and I swear, she knows I'm watching and enjoys it, putting extra sway in her hips as she shimmies into her slacks. The only awkward moment comes when she glances around, and I instantly know she's looking for her firearm. I wonder what happened in her life to make her think of a gun as an extension of her body.

I sit on the corner of the desk as she tucks her tee shirt into her pants. I cut to the chase. Small talk isn't my forte. "Why are you really here, Roxi?"

She tenses. She's been waiting for the question, I can see it in the way her face tightens, and her eyes flick around the room.

I brace for the hammer to drop, because there's *always* a hammer.

She takes a deep breath and exhales roughly, giving me an overly bright smile. "So…" she clears her throat. "I'm your new bar manager."

It takes a full minute for her words to sink in. I hold up a finger. "Wait." I shake my head, still not fully comprehending. "*What?* Lisa's not due for another couple of months."

"Actually, her due date is in a month, and she should have called you?"

I have no idea if she's called me. "I haven't exactly been in a position to check my phone," I snap, hiding my embarrassment with aggression. I stalk out of the office and down the hall to the stockroom, where I dropped my bag. I snatch it up and fumble for my phone as I return to the office, making sure to shut the door behind me. Sure enough, it looks like Lisa called three times, and sent half a dozen texts. The short of it corroborating Roxi's story. She went into early labor and called the bar-sub agency to send someone.

Fuck. *Fuck. Fuck. Fuck.*

"You'll have to go back." I say with a determined scowl.

She looks taken aback. "Why?"

"Because I don't fuck my employees," I shout, coming perilously close to losing my shit completely. And if she's not working for me, then maybe I can convince her to see me again.

Her eyes go wide, then narrow with determination. "I have no problem keeping it in my pants."

"That's not the point," I grit.

"Then what is?" She crosses her arms, pushing her tits

up in the process. "You got a problem with these?" She glances down at her rack, effectively calling me out.

"Not at all. But we've already crossed lines that are unacceptable in employee-boss relationships."

"It sounds like the problem's yours. I have no problem controlling myself."

"Or not seeing me again?"

Regret briefly flashes in her eyes, but then it's replaced with resolve. "I need this job."

My mouth pulls tight and I shake my head. "This is a demanding job that requires discretion and talent."

"And?"

"I'm demanding. Ask Lisa. I'm a mean boss. Long hours, little thanks."

She scoffs, rolling her eyes. "You sound like every boss I've ever had."

"I only work with the best."

She rolls her shoulders back, eyes challenging me. "I am the best."

"Prove it."

"With or without my clothes on?" She teases, arching a brow.

I growl. "Get behind the bar and make me an Old Fashioned." A proper old fashioned that shows off the whiskey used is the mark of a good bartender.

She makes a face and *flounces* out the door, hips swaying with extra swagger. Jesus fucktits. I've got to figure out how to get her out of my bar and into my bed, because this working together shit won't fly. She marches behind the bar, grabs a tumbler and a shaker, setting them both extra-hard on the counter. Slamming is more like it. She examines our selection of premium whiskeys — her first test. All of them are too fine to pollute with a cocktail. She pulls the house whiskey, *my* whiskey, from the bottom shelf. I'll give her points for buttering up her new boss. She drops a sugar cube into the shaker, along with a splash of Grand Marnier. Interesting choice, but I keep an open mind. She adds angostura bitters and muddles. Then she adds the whiskey, ice, and shakes it like a goddamned pro. She's got flare, I'll give her that — like only people who've worked in New York or Vegas have. She drops a large square ice-cube in the cocktail glass, peels part of a lemon and lines the rim. I cross my arms. I'd never add lemon, but I'll wait to taste it. She pours out the cocktail, then peels off a fat slice of orange rind. To my surprise, she holds it over the glass with a lighter, flames it and drops it into the glass, finishing it off with an Amarena cherry.

She slides it across the bar with a satisfied grin. "Try it."

I take a hefty sip. It's… delicious. The lemon is a bright twist and brings out more citrus notes in the whiskey. The Grand Marnier adds a layer of both sweet and bitter that is supremely pleasing. I could drink six of these. Which makes my conundrum even worse — she's good. Maybe even better than Lisa. But she *can't* stay. "Where'd you learn to bartend like that?

"Vegas."

I was right. That also means there has to be a record of her someplace. "How'd you end up here?"

She shrugs and begins to clean up. "I was ready for a change."

"That's a bullshit answer, and we both know it."

She freezes, bar towel inside the shaker.

I pounce. "How come I can't find a record of you anywhere, Roxi? It's like you don't exist."

"Maybe your vetting skills need polishing."

"And maybe you're full of shit." I lean over the bar.

"Are you a fed? Is that why I can't find a trace of you anywhere? No social media, no work records, nothing."

She turns, eyes flashing. "Some of us stay off social for personal reasons. Are you on social?"

I'm not, and the way she poses the question makes me wonder if she looked for me, too.

When I don't answer, she continues. "Maybe some of us don't want to be found. By *anyone*."

The way she spits out the word 'anyone' jars something loose inside me. I give myself a mental slap. "Whoever he is. I'll keep you safe," I declare, giving in to my deepest protective instincts.

She stares at me through stormy eyes, mouth tight. "Thank you, but I can take care of myself."

My stomach sinks to my toes. I'm not about to let her out of my sight, which means she's staying. And my dick is going to fall off from wanting but not having. Danny Pendergast — dickless wonder. Harrison and Stockton will never let me live it down if they get wind of it.

I'm so screwed.

Chapter Seven

"*Well*, well, well, what have we here?" Vincent Ferrari's voice calls from the entrance.

On the other side of the bar, Roxi freezes, as if she recognizes Vince. But she recovers so quickly, most people wouldn't have even noticed. But I'm not most people, and my spidey senses are already on high alert. It's an effort to raise a hand in greeting. "Good to see you, Vince. What can I do for you?" I keep my voice even. "Roxi, this is one of our members, Vince Ferrari. Can you pour him a glass of the reserve? Top shelf on the left."

She nods, avoiding looking at either of us.

Ferrari, on the other hand, can't keep his eyes off Roxi. He looks like a big bad wolf ready to pounce on unsuspecting prey. For a second, I rethink telling Roxi she can't carry in the bar. It takes all my self-control to play it cool, when what I want more than anything is to pound my chest and piss all over the bar, marking my territory.

Roxi turns around, drink in hand and passes it to Ferrari. "Didn't I see you at one of the poker tables at the Nelson a few weeks ago?"

She shrugs noncommittally. "I was there."

"And you bartend, too," he says in a voice laced with suspicion.

I step closer to him, ushering him away from the bar. "My hire, my business." I lead him to the far corner to a pair of leather wingbacks in front of a fireplace. "How long you back in town for?"

Vince gives me an assessing look, but there's something hard and calculating in it that makes my blood run cold. "Depends on the outcome of a few projects I'm working on."

I nod, wishing I had a tumbler myself. God knows I could use a hit of whiskey. But I don't drink when I'm on the job. I make a point of being the sharpest mind in the room, otherwise people get hurt. I learned that the hard way, once upon a time. We make small talk until my skin crawls.

"I should apologize for Ivo," Vince says after a brief silence.

I shake my head. "Nothing to apologize for."

"I don't know what came over him."

"I don't know either. But you know I don't give second chances." I look him straight in the eye. "I'm sure you can relate."

Vince's jaw ticks, but he flashes a smile. "Of course, of course. In our line of work, one must take... precautions."

My stomach churns at the thought he considers my work to be remotely like his. But I don't correct him. Money is money. Business is business.

"I'd like to set up another poker game."

I nod. "Anytime."

"Thursday evening?"

"Eleven okay?"

He nods, tapping his finger against the side of the glass. "I have some special clients coming in. I'd like… her," he nods toward Roxi. "Roxi is it? To deal?"

I take a very slow breath and count to six, pushing aside the red that has clouded my vision. Every cell in my body screams danger. I want to boot him from the club, break his face. "I'm afraid I can't do that," I say evenly with a shake of my head.

Vince's eyes narrow. "Why not?"

"My bartenders are off-limits. Overseeing private poker is outside of the job description."

"Lisa was never off-limits," he accuses with a hint of a snarl.

Lisa has dealt for me on the rare occasion I had a bigger fire to put out, and I trust her implicitly. But I don't owe Vince any explanation. I do however, need to make it very clear that Roxi is off-limits. Permanently. "Lisa was never my girlfriend," I state blandly, as if banging my employee is the most natural thing in the world.

Vince's eyes go wide, and he darts a glance to the bar, then back to me. "I'm surprised, Danny. It's not like you to mix business and pleasure. In all the years I've known you…" His voice trails off as his mouth turns down into a scowl.

I lift a shoulder, keeping my face neutral. "Things change." I lean forward. "Your game will be ready. Back room like always. No players allowed in before ten-thirty or after ten-forty-five. And I'll need the list by tomorrow so I can vet them."

He cocks his head. "Tightening control?"

"Just want to make sure we don't have a repeat of a few weeks ago. It's bad for business."

He nods. "Yes. Of course."

I rise and extend my hand. "May I take your glass?"

Vince is smart enough to recognize the cue that it's time to leave. He hands me his glass and rises, following me to the bar. On the spur of the moment, I duck behind the counter, and sling an arm around Roxi's waist. She turns startled, and I take her chin and kiss her very slowly. Thoroughly. She softens in my arms, relaxing immediately into the kiss. I break it and glance Vince's direction.

The cold, calculating expression has returned to his face, but he covers it with a smile. "You are a fortunate man, Danny."

"I am, aren't I?" We both know I've won this round. "I'll let you see yourself out. Until Thursday?"

He nods once. "Until Thursday."

Roxi waits until the door clicks shut behind Vince before whirling on me. "What in the hell was that for?"

"Thank you for playing along."

She narrows her eyes. "That didn't answer my question. Before Vince What'shisface came in you had a stick up your ass about *employee-boss relationships.*" She uses air quotes. "And then next thing I know, you're kissing me in front of one of your members?" She crosses her arms and leans a hip against the bar. "What's going on?"

How do I explain my gut-level reaction to Vince? Or how I think Vince wants to... acquire her? The whole thing has me spooked. "From here on out, if anyone asks, you're my girlfriend."

Her eyebrows disappear into her hairline. *"Are you fucking kidding me?"* A flush creeps up her neck. "No. Way. It's one thing for us to have sneaky time, but I am most definitely *not* your girlfriend."

"It's for your own safety."

"I think we've already established I can handle myself."

"You have no idea who you're dealing with here."

"Don't I?" She steps into my space, poking a finger into my chest. "I don't think you have an idea who *you're* dealing with. Follow me." She steps around me and rounds the end of the bar. "Well?"

I remain put. "What's this about?"

"Me proving to you once and for all that I can handle it if things get hinky. Come. Here."

I let out an exasperated sigh. I've never met someone so stubborn. "Fine."

"Grab me from behind," she says when I round the corner of the bar.

"You gonna go all Crouching Tiger on me?"

"Just grab me from behind."

I step behind her and wrap her in a bear hug from behind. The next thing I know I'm flat on my back staring at the ceiling with a knee in my sternum and a hand at my throat. "What the fuck?" I sputter. "How'd you do that?"

"Just so we're clear. I can handle myself, and I won't hesitate to use any means at my disposal to stay safe." Her voice is as sharp as a razor.

"Someone hurt you, didn't they?" I growl. "Give me a name. I swear, I will take him down, whoever he is."

Her face twists in agony, before she shakes her head. "Someone I love was... hurt."

Relief floods my body. "Say the word, Roxi. I have connections."

"That's what I'm afraid of," she says so softly, I almost miss it. But then her wide smile is back and she's offering me a hand up. "See? I was right about you being a big teddy bear."

I shake my head with a guttural noise. "Never. And you don't know the kinds of people you'll be dealing with here.

Not all of them are… honorable. So as long as you're working here, you're going to let people think you're my girlfriend."

"Or what?"

I open my hands. "Or you don't work here."

Chapter Eight

*H*er indignant gasp is almost enough to make me laugh — if her safety wasn't on the line.

"Just so I'm clear. First, I couldn't work here because we've fucked. Now I can't work here *if I'm not your girlfriend?* You're insane. Has anybody told you that?"

I nod, completely at home with my hypocrisy. "Every day."

"And you don't feel the need to be, er... consistent with your rules?"

"My business, my rules."

"Rules are shit if you're not consistent."

"My rules change based on circumstances. And... thanks to Vince, we have an unusual set of circumstances to deal with. So take it or leave it. You can stay here and pretend to be my girlfriend, or you can go back to the temp agency."

I swear a look of sheer panic flickers across her face, but it happens so fast, I can't be sure, because in the next instant her gaze bores straight into me. "I'll agree on one condition."

"Name it."

"No. Sex."

Now it's my turn to be surprised. "That's your condition?"

"I don't do relationships, and since this is a pretend relationship it needs to be fully pretend. And I trust you'll only kiss me when absolutely necessary."

Her conditions take the wind out of my sails, but at least this way she'll stay safe, and that's my number one job where my employees are concerned — keeping them safe at all costs. I stick out my hand. "Deal." We shake, and when our hands separate, I feel the loss of her touch all the way to my bones. "First things first, let me give you the tour."

Surprisingly, the day passes quickly. Roxi's a quick study, and it's obvious she's experienced. By late afternoon, I've had three texts from Lisa with pictures of a scrunch-faced newborn with black eyes and hair peeking out from a blanket.

It's a girl!!!!

I swipe to the next picture — of Lisa looking tired and happy, holding the little thing. The caption brings a lump to my throat.

I named her Polly Danielle.

I shoot back a text: *Are you sure you want to do that?*

Dots appear, and in a few seconds she responds. *Of course, silly. Don't be a dumbass. She's your goddaughter.*

I resolve to redouble my efforts to learn who the father is. Lisa has been uncharacteristically tight-lipped, and my research has turned up nothing. Maybe Roxi's right, and I need to polish my vetting skills. I send off another text.

I'll stop by the hospital after work. I type more. *Whoever he is, he doesn't deserve the two of you.* But I erase that part. Lisa knows how I feel about the douchebag who knocked her up, and I don't want to diminish her happiness.

It's slow tonight, and I decide to close the Den at nine-thirty so I can get to the hospital at a decent hour. The benefit of owning a private club where I determine the hours. It's not like I'm unreachable. If someone's desperate for me to open, they have my number.

I walk back to my office and take in the desk with not a little regret. But we've made our choices, and it's for the best. I can't afford the liability of feelings. I tuck my laptop into my satchel and grab Roxi's holster from the drawer. I double check the door's locked when I step into the hall. "I'll drive you home," I say as I hand over her weapon.

She bends and attaches it to her left ankle. "No need. I drove myself."

"No can do. Oscar can drive it to your place and give you the keys tomorrow."

She purses her lips. "So now you're holding me captive?"

"Not at all. But everyone knows I'd never let my girl-friend drive herself home alone."

She rises, glaring daggers. "Fine. Whatever you say."

"Keys?"

She digs in her purse and drops the car keys into my outstretched hand, and marches ahead of me toward the door.

"Oscar, will you make sure Ms. Rickoli's car gets deliv-ered to her residence tonight? You can bring the keys with you tomorrow."

"Sure thing, boss."

"Thank you. I'll text you the address."

Roxi bristles all the way to my car, but stands aside to let me open the door for her.

"Where to?" I ask as I pull onto Gennessee.

"West Side." It's an eclectic neighborhood, and not far from my condo in the Crossroads, which I like. "What time should I report tomorrow?" She asks when I pull up to the address.

"Two. I can handle things before then."

"Great." She brings a hand to the door.

"Wait. Let me." I hop out of my Lotus and race around the front to open her door. As she takes my hand, the hair on my neck stands up. I scan up and down the street but don't see anything unusual. No cars idling or people loitering. Still, it feels like we're being watched. I keep hold of her hand while I shut the car door. "I'm going to walk you to your door," I say in a low voice. "And when we get to the porch, I'm going to put my arms around you and we're going to kiss. Understand?"

She picks up on the urgency in my voice. "Everything okay?"

"I just want to make sure."

She gives my hand a squeeze and leans into my arm, clasping my bicep. "How does this look?"

"Like you're totally into me."

"Cocky bastard," she mutters so only I can hear.

"Definitely."

"This your place?" I stop in front of a modern two-story house comprised of metal and cement. "Fancy digs," I say when we land on the porch.

"I'm housesitting."

"Ahh. Of course. So you're not going to invite me in?"

She shakes her head with an amused smile. "I promised my girlfriend I'd limit the shenanigans to the front porch."

A breeze dances through the porch, rustling the tree leaves between the houses. I tuck a stray lock behind her ear. She tilts up her face, eyes sparkling with expectation. I wrap an arm around the small of her back, pulling her close, and slide my hand underneath her hair to the base of her skull.

She meets me halfway. At first the kiss is tentative, forced. I brush my mouth against hers, giving her space. She wraps an arm around my shoulder with a sigh, and instantly, she melts, her body becomes soft, lips pliant. I deepen the kiss, licking at the inside of her lip. Her tongue darts out to meet mine. It acts like a spark to a powder keg, and suddenly we're a tangle of lips, tongues, teeth, little moans and licks, grinding through our clothes until we pull apart, breathless. She's flushed, eyes bright with desire.

"Are you sure I can't come in?" I can't help but ask, dropping another kiss to the corner of her mouth.

"I'm sure," she says firmly.

I step back, not bothering to cover the bulge in my pants. Let her see what her kisses do to me. "Promise you'll lock your door?"

She rolls her eyes. "Of *course*. And—"

"I know, I know. You can take care of yourself. Let me guess, you sleep with your pistol under your pillow, too," I state rhetorically. Given what I've seen of her, I'd be surprised if she didn't.

She snorts. "Wouldn't you love to find out?" She presses a last kiss on my mouth and slips inside.

I stay put until I hear the lock snick into place. Back in the car, I wait to turn on the engine until I see the lights on the second story flick on. I can't shake the feeling we were watched, but I can't stay here all night, either. With a shake of my head, I turn the key and the engine roars to life. I make a quick stop at the twenty-four hour grocery in Westport for flowers and a pink plushie before heading to the maternity ward at St. Luke's by the Plaza. The nurse waves me back, mentioning that Lisa had let them know I was on my way up.

I knock on the door, then push it open. I'm surprised to see Harrison and Stockton lounging in the chairs, surrounded by an explosion of pink balloons, flowers and an enormous teddy bear. "I see someone's beat me to the punch," I say wryly as I enter and drop a kiss on Lisa's cheek. "Congratulations. Can I see my little namesake?"

"You'll have to fight them," she tilts her chin to Harrison and Stockton, and I spy a tiny bundle in Harrison's massive arms. "They've been fighting over Polly since they got here two hours ago."

"For real?" I can't imagine either of them baby crazy. Or myself, but my heart starts to pound erratically when I approach and stare down at the most perfect face I've ever seen. "Hand her over," I say gruffly.

"Are you sure you're up for that?" teases Lisa.

I nod, unable to speak for the sudden lump in my throat. Harrison lays her in my arms, she hardly weighs anything. Her eyes are shut, but dark lashes brush against cheeks, her nose is a little button, her mouth a perfect little bow, and she makes the tiniest cooing sigh as she settles into the crook of my elbow. Dark brows frame her face, and I can see a shock of black hair peeping out from underneath the little beanie on her head. My heart hurts with the beauty of this little being.

"Don't let them fool you," Lisa calls over from where she's propped up on the bed. "They bawled like babies when they first met her."

I flash her a grin, grateful for her understanding. "She's perfect, Lisa."

Lisa returns my smile with such motherly pride that my chest pulls tight. "Isn't she? I feel like the luckiest person alive."

"You'll both have whatever you need," I promise. I'm serious, too. All the things I had to scrap for? They're little Polly's. And she won't even have to ask.

"Hey, we're helping too," calls Stockton. He looks from me, to Harrison, and then to Lisa. "He doesn't get to steal our thunder just because he got here late."

"I got here as fast as I could," I protest. "I had to train Lisa's replacement."

"My sub," she corrects. "I'm planning on coming back."

"That's right," Harrison agrees with a nod of his head. "No one can replace you."

I look down at Polly sleeping peacefully in my arms. I'd never get anything done if she was mine. I'd be content to sit and stare all day. "You're irreplaceable to Polly, first. And yes, your job's waiting for you whenever you're ready to come back. Even if it's six months from now."

"Roxi was that good, huh?" she says with a little pout.

"She'll manage."

"Wait. *Roxi?*" Harrison's eyes light. "The dame from the Nelson? She's your temp?" He drops his head back with a laugh. "You better start looking for new work, Lise," he says. "Danny was all over her shit."

"Was not," I retort.

"Look me in the eye and tell me you haven't tapped that. I saw the look in your eye when you saw her dancing with that old geezer."

I lie straight to his face. "You know how I feel about mixing business and sex."

"I also know it's high time you revisited that rule. When are you going to live for you and not all the people that you've decided it's your responsibility to look out for?"

I wave a hand. "It's not that many."

"Isn't it?" Stockton chimes in, counting on his fingers. "First, there's your mom. Then the Anderssons."

"Don't forget Alison Walker," Harrison adds.

"Lisa and Poppy."

"And who knows how many others," Harrison finishes. "When are you going to realize you can't atone for your family's sins by rescuing every damsel in distress you run across? Who's going to look out for you?"

"Isn't that a little bit of the pot calling the kettle black?" I toss back. "Sadly, there are a lot of assholes in the world, and a lot of women who've been hurt by said assholes. Why would I sit on my fortune when I could help someone?" Polly squirms in my arms and I lower my voice. "You both were born with everything. Do you have any idea how hard it is on the East side of town? Where you have to scratch and scrape for scraps? Do you have any idea how much it would have helped my family if someone, *anyone*, had noticed mom was in trouble? Maybe she could have gotten out before it cost her everything." Polly squirms and lets out a tiny cry. I return her to her mother's arms, doing my best to ignore the awkward silence my outburst has caused.

Harrison spreads his hands. "You're a good guy, Danny. You've always been straight-up. I just... I just... wanna see you get the girl."

"Guys like me don't get the girl," I say with a shake of my head. "Guys like me get the girl killed. Or maimed."

Which is why I have to send Roxi back to the temp agency first thing tomorrow.

Chapter Nine

*R*oxi storms in promptly at two, brown eyes flashing fire. "Did you think you could get rid of me that easy? I'm just glad there was no one else available. Did it ever occur to you that I have bills to pay?"

"It's for your own good," I growl.

"No. I think it's for *your* own good. We've already established—"

"That you can handle yourself. But you don't know who you're dealing with." She leans across the bar and I catch a whiff of her perfume. It's enough to make my resolve waver.

"I think you're scared," she says quietly, but with steel in her voice. "I think your gangster friend spooked you."

She means to provoke me, and it works. "He's not my friend," I answer with equal steel.

"Of course he's not," she retorts. "But I know how men like you operate. You think if you can't be someone's bodyguard twenty-four-seven, that you've failed." She makes a fist on the counter. "It doesn't work that way, buddy."

"Buddy?"

She lets out an exasperated sigh. "*That's* your take-away? That I called you buddy?"

I lean over the bar, until our faces are mere inches apart. "Like it or not, sweetheart. Now that you're part of the Whiskey Den, you're *my* responsibility. Whether you're at work or not."

"That's crap."

"Is it? I didn't sleep last night, thinking about how vulnerable you are in that house."

"There's an alarm."

"Alarms can be hacked."

"I have protection."

"Last time I checked, no one could aim a gun in their sleep. So unless you're a vampire or you've got some magic juju that lets you never sleep, you're vulnerable."

Her freckles pop into relief as her face pales. "You're that worried?"

"When you're out of my sight, yes."

She makes a noise of disbelief, or maybe surprise. "And you think giving me the boot would keep me safe? That's a logical fallacy. You've just admitted I'm safer here."

She has a point, much to my chagrin. "I hate it when you're right."

Her smile returns. "Get used to it."

I could kiss her. It would be so easy to reach across and bend her head to mine. I've never regretted a deal as much as I do now. But I promised.

Behind us, a voice clears her throat. Roxi whirls, and I catch sight of white blonde curls. "Emmaline?"

She throws herself into a chair with a sob. "Oh Danny, I've made such a mess of things."

I know what this looks like, and Roxi's expression confirms the worst. "You. Stay," I order as I round the bar and pull out a chair next to Em. "What is it sweetheart? I know you miss your mom, but Declan—"

"But that's just it," she wails. "I sent him away."

Now I'm confused. "Roxi? Can you bring the reserve bottle and three tumblers?" I pat Emmaline on the back. "Why would you send Declan away, honey? He loves you."

"He does. Look." She hands me an invitation. I don't bother to read it, because there was one waiting in the Whiskey Den mailbox this morning.

Roxi slams the bottle on the table, startling both of us. "If I'm pouring three drinks, WILL SOMEONE TELL ME WHAT'S GOING ON?"

Emmaline looks from me to Roxi and back to me. "Where's Lisa?"

"She had her baby."

This sends Emmaline back into paroxysms of tears. I bite back a groan of frustration. The downside of caring for damsels in distress. I take a tumbler and force it into Emmaline's hands. "Take a breath, then take a drink." I grab a tumbler for myself and drain it. It's not enough to make me loopy, but it will help the telling of the story. "The short story — Emmaline's grandfather was a runner for my great-grandfather, back in the day. He got caught and did time, preferring jail to being labeled a snitch. Tom wrote him when he was in jail and said whatever the Andersson family needed in perpetuity, the Pendergasts would return the favor. Emmaline and her mother found the note when her father was in nursing care for Alzheimer's. So of course I helped them out. And again, when Em's mother developed the disease."

Roxi's expression is carefully neutral and I can't get a read off her at all. "Wow. That's quite a story."

"Mama and I would have been sunk without Danny,"

Emmaline says, wiping her eyes. "He was my first investor when I started Madame M Lingerie."

Roxi's eyes go wide. "*You're* Madame M?" She looks to me for verification, and I nod. She lets out a slow whistle.

"I still don't understand why you sent Declan away."

Emmaline hiccups. "I was scared, and-and I thought I was doing him a favor, but I've made a mess of everything." Her lower lip trembles as tears threaten to spill out again.

"From the looks of the invitation, it doesn't look like he's given up. Are you going to go?"

"What's the worst that could happen?" Roxi asks.

"That I could die old, crazy, and alone," says Emmaline.

"If you love him, you should go," she encourages softly.

I nod in agreement, deciding right then that I'm going, too, and that Roxi's coming with me.

Chapter Ten

*R*oxi glares at me. "For the last time, I'm not going."

I glare back. "For the last time, you *are.*"

"I can handle the bar on my own."

"I'm sure you can. But no one runs the Den without me."

I tap the suitcase with my toe. "I packed everything you need." I swear she mutters 'chauvinist' under her breath. "That may be. But you're getting on that plane with me, and we're already late." At least the airport is right down the road, and the flight crew will wait.

"And what if I don't?"

I love her sass. It's a total fucking turn-on. But right now, it's irritating as fuck. "I will not hesitate to throw your ass over my shoulder and carry you to the plane."

Her eyes narrow. "Don't forget, I can drop you."

"Don't forget, I will not hesitate to spank that pretty ass of yours."

Her eyes light with hunger. It's been agony, the last two weeks, wanting but not touching. I've caught her staring as much as she's caught me. We've kissed only twice — once before the poker game I organized for Vince, and again the other day, when an associate of his popped in for a late dinner. Both times left us grouchy, and very much wanting more. I could see it in her eyes, hear it in the groan of frustration she didn't bother to hide.

I press my advantage. "If you don't go, I guarandamntee you Vince will get wind of it and our little deal will be exposed for the lie it is."

"I'll lay low this weekend."

"Don't be so foolish as to think he's not having the house you're staying in watched."

"Why would he do that?"

"Because he wants what he can't have, and if he sees an opening, he'll take it."

"You give him too much credit," she scoffs. "Besides —" Her voice turns hard as ice. "I will not hesitate to drop him or anyone else."

"And I don't want it to come to that." We stare each other down. I play my last card. My voice drops. "What are you afraid of, Roxi?" I step around the suitcase until I'm so close I can feel her breath skate across my cheek.

"Nothing."

Her voice says otherwise.

"Are you afraid we might… break our rules?"

Her breath catches, but she shakes her head. "I'm not afraid of anything."

"Liar." I bend my head to nuzzle the hollow below her ear. "I promise what happens in Napa will stay in Napa."

A shiver ripples through her. "Yes," she whispers in an almost pained voice. "I'll go."

I step away with a triumphant grin. "See? How hard was that?"

She lets out a growl of pure frustration, but I see the

smile pulling at the corner of her mouth. "You'll pay for that," she promises.

"I hope so. But right now, we're late for the plane."

I grab our bags and head through the door. "Call if something comes up," I say to Oscar as we step outside.

"Don't worry, boss. I've got security on it twenty-four-seven."

"Good man."

In less than ten minutes, I pull into a reserved spot at the downtown airport. The jet sits on the tarmac, engines already idling. "We're using Steele Conglomerate's plane?"

"We all went in on it. None of us use it enough on our own to retain a full-time crew. But together, we do."

"I see. But why the Kansas City Kings logo beneath it?"

"Harrison and Stockton and a couple of friends of theirs put together the partnership to buy the team a year ago and keep it here in Kansas City."

Roxi's eyes widen. "Wow. I gotta tell my dad. He'll go crazy. He used to take me to farm league games when I was a little kid."

"Let me know when he comes to visit, and we'll go to a game." It's a stupid offer to make, because Opening Day is five months away, but it's worth it to see the smile on her face. I drop the luggage at the foot of the stairs and take Roxi's hand to lead her up, but I stop short.

"What is it?"

I turn and give her a hard stare. "Your weapon."

She looks confused. "What about it?"

"Are you licensed to carry in California?"

She opens her mouth to speak, then snaps it shut. It's the first time I've seen her genuinely flustered. "Doesn't matter," she finally says with a shrug.

"What do you mean it doesn't matter?"

She glares at me and lowers her voice. "It doesn't matter because neither of us are going to say anything to the flight crew, nor to anyone else."

"But you could go to jail."

"Funny thing for you to say, Mr. Poker Night."

"Is it really worth risking jail?"

"Yes," she says with so much ice in her voice, I shudder.

"I swear if I ever meet whoever made you so scared." I let the remainder of the threat hang between us.

"See, when you say stuff like that, I know you're a big teddy bear."

I lace my fingers through hers. "Am not."

"Are."

"Not."

"Whiskey, Mr. Pendergast?" the flight attendant asks when we take our seats.

"And one for Ms. Rickoli as well," I answer with a nod.

As soon as we're buckled and our drinks have been served, the jet barrels down the runway and shoots into the air, banking hard so that we see downtown from the window.

"So let me see if I can keep this straight," Roxi says after draining her glass. "You went to Stanford with the Case brothers."

I nod.

"And the Steele Conglomerate guys."

"Yep," I say with another nod.

"But that's only seven, and you said you all rowed in an eight man boat together?"

"Only my senior year, and it wasn't all of us. It was me, Austin, Declan, Stockton, Harrison, Owen, Jackson, and Mac. Austin and Dec were freshman, but they had grit and made it onto the varsity boat. We won the national championships that year. Smoked Harvard," I say with a smile.

"Why'd you quit rowing?"

The question I hate answering most. I push out of my chair and make myself a heavy pour at the bar. I return to my seat and for a long moment, stare out the window at the puffy clouds below us.

Roxi drops a hand to my knee. "If it's too painful, you don't have to talk about it."

I drain the glass in three gulps, wincing at the burn, drawing strength from the pain. "Nah. It's been ten years. I should be able to talk about it." But time has a way of shrinking when death is involved, and when I shut my eyes, the grief slices across my belly. "I had a girlfriend. Her name was Anita. She was crazy as fuck. Super smart, super passionate. Prone to dramatic outburst. Sometimes I think she was bi-polar, but nobody knew it." I can still see her doe brown eyes, and her high cheekbones, and the curly hair she kept short and wild, just like her personality.

"We'd planned to take a month and hike Italy after graduation. But after our stunning win against Harvard, all of us in the boat got invited to National Selection Camp for the Olympics. It was the first time an entire boat had been invited, and we had visions of the days when collegiate boats dominated at the Olympics."

I lean back and shut my eyes for a second, reliving the euphoria when we learned all of us were going to the trials. "It was a real 'all for one and one for all' moment. We felt like nothing could stop us. The last time a collegiate boat had been to the Olympics was '68. The last time a collegiate boat won gold was '56. We were convinced it was our time."

"But something happened."

"Anita happened." I state flatly, no longer feeling

anything about her except empty. "She was pissed because it meant canceling our trip to Italy. Hysterical. She refused to see reason, and we fought. A big ugly fight, and ultimately, she got in her car and drove away, and right into a semi."

Roxi gasps, and I open my eyes to see her hand covering her mouth.

"I guess the good thing was that she was killed instantly. But her family blamed me, and that was that." I tap my fingers on the side of my glass. "Killed any love I had for the sport right then and there."

"But your teammates—"

"Understood. They went, but none made it past the third cut. The team's spirit was broken. I think Harrison and Stockton continue to row because they're still chasing that feeling, the euphoria of a perfectly balanced boat on the water."

"I'm so sorry, Danny. That must have been indescribably awful for you."

"I've endured worse," I say with a wry smile.

She stares at me a long moment, eyes full of pain. "I can only imagine."

It's not my place to ask, but I get the distinct feeling she understands what I mean.

Chapter Eleven

_I_'ve booked us at a B&B in Yountville, twenty-five minutes down Mt. Veeder from where Declan's vineyard is located. Emmaline meets us for drinks in the living room as soon as we arrive, bristling with nervous energy. "I should call Declan right now, shouldn't I? Maybe I should drive up tonight."

I hand her a glass of Pinot Noir. "You're overthinking this. Go upstairs, take a bath and book yourself into a spa for the day tomorrow."

"I'd love to join you," Roxi adds with a warm smile. "I haven't indulged in girlie activities in ages. I'm overdue."

I shoot her a grateful smile. Maybe it's her confidence or her fierce independence, or maybe it's because there's no expectation for anything between us, but her lack of jealousy as she's learned about the people, _the women_ I've helped with my fortune, has surprised me. Just when I expect her to zig, she zags. Her reactions keep me off-balance, disconcerted, even. It's almost like she's proud of me. But I chalk up my observations as wishful thinking because there's plenty in my life to _not_ be proud of.

"I'd like that, too," says Emmaline. "I was an only, so I never had sisters to do girlie things with."

Pain flashes across Roxi's face, but it's gone before Emmaline notices. "This will be special then." To anyone else's ears, her comment seems completely normal. But I notice the tightness in her voice, like her throat has closed. I want to ask her about it. Curiosity is burning a hole in my gut, but until she says something, I'm keeping my questions to myself. Whatever burden she's carrying, it the kind of deep shit that has to be volunteered, and it won't be shared lightly. With anyone. A tiny flicker of hope rises in my chest. Could Roxi ever see me as a safe place? A landing place for her deepest secrets?

The valet returns with our room key. "Sir, I've delivered your suitcases. You'll find everything is as you requested."

I tip him, and motion to Roxi. "You hungry?" I ask as I lead her up the grand staircase and down the hall to our suite.

"Famished, now that I think about it."

I slip the key into the lock and turn the handle. "Good. I took the liberty of ordering in."

She takes four steps into the suite and turns around, eyes wide, mouth dropped open. "Are you for real kidding me?"

A spot in my chest warms and spreads across my torso. "Do you like it?"

She gives me a look that can only be described as *fucking duh*. "Uhh… *yeah*. You'd have to be crazy not to love it."

The suite *is* incredible. The focal point is a king-sized bed with a French blue bedspread and crisp white pillows. To the left as we enter is an enormous en suite, which I hope she'll explore later. Across from the bed is a sitting area with a couch, coffee table and two wingbacks. But the *piece de resistance* are the French doors that open onto a wide balcony that overlooks row upon row of vines. Dinner has been laid out on the patio furniture, and in another hour the sun will be setting.

"Shall I pour wine?"

"Wait." She bends and removes her holster, slipping it into a drawer. "I won't be needing this."

The warm spot in my chest flares as I offer her a glass of bubbly rosé.

She clinks her glass to mine. "Thank you. I already feel my blood pressure dropping."

"The pleasure is all mine." I pull out a seat for her, and for the next hour ply her with food and wine as the sun drops lower in the sky. The conversation is easy, relaxed. As if we were friends, not boss and employee fighting sexual tension every second of the day. The light is perfect — warm and golden, and her hair glows like a halo. "I never realized you had so much gold in your hair," I blurt, unable to keep my observation to myself.

Her laugh is sweetly musical, and a shot of awareness rocks through me. "Are you flirting with me Danny?"

"Only a little," I admit.

She drains the last of her wine. "Can I ask you something?"

"I figured I'd take the couch," I offer, hoping to head off any awkward conversation.

She stares at me, an amused smile flirting with the corner of her mouth. "You think that's what I wanted to talk about?"

My stomach drops, then jumps to my throat, then drops again. I recognize that seductive tone of voice. How could I forget it? It's burned into my ears from our first night together. I swallow, unable to find my voice. "Unlucky guess," I manage to rasp after a minute.

She shakes her head, making a funny noise in her throat, somewhere between a laugh and a snort. I'm taken aback by the look in her eyes when our gazes tangle. Her amber eyes glow with an intensity that's arresting. Deeply arousing. My heart tries to punch a hole in my chest as it takes off to the races. The air between us feels heavy with unspoken words. "Why this?" she finally asks, gesturing in front of us.

I freeze, torn between a bullshit answer and the truth. The bullshit answer sits on my tongue, eager to fly from my mouth. It's my stock answer, my bulletproof vest, so to speak. But I don't want that. Not with Roxi. A wave of nausea sweeps through my stomach. I don't confess my true feelings to anyone. It's been so long, I can't remember what it's like. Heat races up my spine. I take her hand, twining my fingers with hers. "I wanted this to be special. For you to have something nice to remember. I..." My mouth is dry as ash, and my cheeks are flaming. "I wanted to spoil you." For an awful second, I think I'm going to vomit, but hell if I'm going to let that happen. I gulp down the last of my wine. Fuck sipping it like a civilized person, I need to save face.

"*Danny*," she says, squeezing my hand. "Will you look at me?"

Her eyes are soft when I meet her gaze. Shining. "You really are a big, sweet, gooey teddy bear, aren't you?"

I bite back a laugh. "Absolutely not."

"I'll always know better." She rises, pulling my hand around her back when I stand too. "When you said what happens in Napa stays in Napa..." Her eyelashes flutter down.

"Yes, what about it?" The air between us crackles. My

cells buzz everywhere our bodies touch, from our thighs, to our hands, to her tits pressed against my chest. Every instinct shouts to kiss her, to devour her plump mouth and taste the wine I'm certain still lingers on her tongue. But I hold back, hoping… for what exactly, I don't know. But the flame glows brightly in my chest as I hold my breath waiting for her next move.

"Does it have to stay in Napa?" Her voice cracks a little, as if she's nervous in the asking.

The flame in my chest roars to life, as if gasoline were poured on it. Some dark, secret part of me has been waiting for this. Hoping. I drop my head and nip a trail from her ear to the hollow at the base of her neck. "We'd be breaking all sorts of rules."

"I know." Her voice is husky, breathless.

"People would talk."

"I know."

"You could get hurt." And so could I.

She sighs heavily. "I know. But I can't stop wanting you. Or dreaming about you. I… I don't care about the consequences."

"Are you sure? Because once we cross this line, there's no going back."

"I'm pretty sure we crossed this line the day we met," she says in a breathless rush. "I want you, Danny. I want your hands on me, your mouth on me, and I want to make love to you all night long in a real bed."

Chapter Twelve

I devour Roxi in the deepest kind of claiming kiss, a kiss that sets fire to our souls. I intend to take my time tasting every inch of her, but right now, I'm content with exploring her mouth, tasting the wine that remains on her tongue. She molds herself to me, and I lose myself in the sweet sensations swirling through my body. I'm light, and energy, heat and hope. In this moment everything, *everything* seems possible.

Somehow, we make our way through the French doors and to the bed, kicking off shoes and peeling off pants and shirts, then undergarments until we collapse onto the bed in a tangle of limbs. Roxi giggles, and the sound is like butterflies and angels and magic all wrapped into one. It takes a moment for me to recognize it as happiness. She's happy. And the lightness buzzing inside me, tingling my toes, fluttering in my chest, that must be happiness too, because I sure as hell am not having an aneurysm.

I frame her face, threading my fingers through her hair, and I kiss the freckles splashed across her cheeks, her eyelids, the line of her jaw, until she whimpers and I return home to the wide, plump mouth that I could spend the rest of my life kissing.

I crawl over her, resting my knees on either side of her hips, and I stare down at her, marveling at the way her hair splays across the comforter, the way her eyes sparkle with delight and anticipation. I've never known a woman to embrace sex the way she does. "I'm not sure where to start," I say. "I want to kiss all of you."

"That depends," she says with a coy smile. "Are you a dessert first, kind of man? Or an eat your vegetables first kind of man?"

I drop to my elbows and nip at her collarbone. "I'm a seven-course farm-to-fork meal with paired wines, a cheese plate, dessert, coffee and liqueur kind of man."

My answer sends her into a paroxysm of giggles. "Sounds like you have a bit of a problem, then." She says, gasping for air.

"I've got it," I say, moving back so that I'm perched at her feet. "I'm a 'this little piggy' kind of guy," I say with a wink, encasing her slender foot in my hand and bringing her toes to my mouth, where I gently kiss each tip. Next, I place a soft kiss at the arch of her foot. Her gasps of laughter quickly turn into moans of delight. Not wanting to ignore her other foot, I repeat myself before moving to her ankle, and caressing her calf. With my mouth, I trace the snake tattoo that winds up her leg, much like I did the first night we were together, but taking infinite care to not miss a spot. By the time I reach her apex, she's panting and squirming, one hand braced against the headboard, the other fisting the comforter.

Roxi drops her knees open, putting herself on display. "You have the prettiest cunt," I say reverently, lightly caressing her slick, swollen folds. "But that is most definitely dessert."

She lets out a throaty groan of frustration as I lightly draw my fingers across the swell of her belly. To my surprise and shock, the words *babymaking belly* pop into my head. I sit with that fantasy a moment, the idea of spilling my seed into her, of creating a life, of watching this gentle curve swell. My cock likes the idea, too. My crown is slick with precome and my cock grows even thicker, bobbing between us. I table the thought for now. Whatever we have is still too new, too fragile to be thinking about children.

With the flat of my tongue I lick a line from her belly button to the valley between her luscious breasts. I take my time devouring each one, noting the slight differences in their shape, the way they fill my hand, the way her nipples pucker and draw up into tight little bullets. I flick my tongue around each areola, memorizing each ridge and bump before drawing a hardened peak into my mouth. She arches off the bed, offering herself up, and I tease and suck at her, marking each breast as my own, while drawing my cock back and forth through her wet folds, coating myself in her desire.

Touching her like this is the sweetest agony. I want it to go on forever. "Let me touch you, too." She begs, scraping her fingernails across my chest, leaving behind a trail of fire.

"You'll get to. I promise. But first you have to let me worship you."

She rocks into my cock with a groan. "You say that like I'm a goddess."

"You are, sweetheart. You are." I kiss a trail back down, pausing to leave a bite mark on her hipbone, and another by the head of the snake. "You're temptation incarnate."

"And the sinning is so good," she says as she sucks in a sharp breath.

"Indeed," I murmur, as I seal my mouth over her mound and suck.

She arches with a guttural moan. "You make me feel so good."

"I'm going to make you fly," I declare before sliding my tongue down her slit and thrusting into her channel. I'm surrounded by the taste of her, the scent of her arousal, the tang of salt on her skin. I tongue her again, thrusting as deep as I can, then sliding up her seam to her clit. She grinds into my face seeking release, egging me on with hedonistic sighs and moans of appreciation. I feast, savoring every drop, licking her until she shatters with a keening cry, thighs gripping my head like a vice as she rocks and thrusts, riding wave after wave of ecstasy.

She hijacks my plans when her eyes fly open. "I want you inside me. Bare. I have an IUD."

My cock twitches eagerly at the thought of being fully encased in her heat with nothing between us. "Are you sure?"

She nods. "I've never wanted anyone like I want you, Danny."

"I've never not used a condom," I confess, warmth spreading across my chest. I'm moved that she trusts me like this.

"Me either," she says, eyes wide, pupils still blown from her orgasm. "I want this, if you do."

"I do," I say, lowering my head to take her mouth in a claiming kiss that leaves me dizzy, drunk on her taste and the emotions running high between us.

My cock is already slick from sliding through her folds, and I pause, teasing the head at her entrance. I can barely focus through the exquisite sensations shooting up my shaft. I shut my eyes, taking a moment to commit this to memory. Then I open my eyes, and catch her watching me through hooded eyes, a languid smile pulling at the corner of her mouth. "Ready?" I murmur.

She nods, smile spreading wide. I take her hand, threading our fingers together, as I slowly stroke into her. It's fucking heaven, the wet, the heat. And it's a million times better with nothing between us. Her eyes grow glazed as we continue to rock together, me angling my hips to slide against her clit, she tilting hers up to allow for deeper penetration. "I feel you so deep inside me," she says, voice strangled.

"You're pure magic, Roxi," I murmur, not taking my eyes off her. The heat between us is so intense, the connection in our gaze, it might kill me if I looked away. Staring into her eyes as I slowly fuck in and out of her is the most erotic thing I've ever experienced. Energy not only races up the back of my legs to pool at the base of my spine, it burns in my chest with the energy of the sun, building and spreading with each stroke, until my body is consumed in the white light of ecstatic fusion. "Do you feel it?" I ask, strokes becoming firmer, rocking deeper. "Do you feel this between us?" I rasp in a voice I don't recognize.

"Yes. Oh god, yes." Her whole body is writhing beneath me, meeting my thrusts with wriggles and squirms. "Oh, Danny, yes." Her mouth opens into an *O* at the same time her body shudders and twitches, and her pussy clenches around my cock in waves so intense, I follow her right over the cliff into oblivion, body seizing as I drive into her as deep as I can, spilling my seed in the deepest part of her in heavy, hard spurts.

My mouth goes numb and I can't feel my fingers. Or my toes. For a brief second, I marvel at the idea of all the blood in my body rushing to my cock. It sure as hell felt that way when my brain exploded with white light.

I collapse onto her, and her arms wrap around me, fingers lightly stroking up my spine. "That was… amazing," she murmurs in a voice so relaxed it almost sounds sleepy. "When can we do that again?"

Chapter Thirteen

———————

 I'm not a 'happy guy' kind of laugher. Sure, I have a sense of humor, but it tends toward the dark, and I'm more often amused with sarcasm and irony. And I sure as fuck don't laugh because I'm happy. I can't even say I know what happiness feels like. The concept of happiness, of relaxing into a state of peace and content-ment is as foreign to me as walking on Mars. So I'm surprised by the laughter that bubbles up from my belly at Roxi's request for a do-over. And even more surprised by the lightness in my chest, the sensation of utter peace that's descended upon me. The recognition of it makes my stomach do somersaults — like I'm standing at the edge of a high dive, or ready to jump out of a plane.

But as I roll to the side and she snuggles into my arm, resting her head on my chest, I push the fear away, because this feels so... good. "I like this," she says with a happy sigh. She lifts her head, the corner of her mouth twitching. "Don't get me wrong, I like the other stuff too, the naughty stuff, but this is... nice."

Her eyes crinkle as she says it, and I can't help but

smile back at her. I nod my agreement. "We can be just as naughty in bed."

"I'm counting on it," she says with lift of her eyebrows.

Her enthusiasm is equal parts infectious and disconcerting. I trace a finger across her cheekbone. "You know what I admire most about you?"

"My hot bod?"

"Oh, I definitely admire that. But I admire your enthusiasm more. The way you jump into whatever's at hand with both feet."

Her gaze wavers and for a second her face crumples with something akin to grief. But I blink and it's gone. "Thank you," she says, voice dropping. I had a good teacher."

"All I learned from the adults in my life was how to strike first and strike hard."

Her gaze jerks to mine. "I can't believe that. There's too much good in you."

I grunt my disagreement. "My great-grandfather was a notorious gangster who lived a double life. On the one hand, he was an upstanding citizen, with a wife and children and a big fancy house on Ward Parkway. On the other — he was a thug who would clip you at the knees, or worse, if you crossed him."

"But that doesn't mean that's your destiny."

"It's hard to get away from." A heavy sigh escapes me. How do I even begin to talk about the burden of carrying Tom's name? "Kansas City… thinks of Tom as some kind of a modern-day Robin Hood who saved us from the Great Depression, who helped the immigrant and the orphan. Fuck, who built the city. But they don't think about the cost — to his family, to the people who disagreed with him… how many innocent people were victimized while he built his empire?"

"But you're doing your part to right those wrongs," she says, laying her palm on my chest. Her movement is meant to be comforting, but it does little to assuage the beast within. Because now that I've started, I can't seem to shut my mouth. All the garbage I've kept inside for years, for my entire fucking life, all of it — the anger, the shame, the hurt, the disappointment, comes spewing out like some kind of a sulfur vent in the earth's crust.

"He went to federal prison for fraud related to his enormous gambling debts. He died with nothing. And by the time I was born, we had less than nothing. The only thing we had was a name, and-and, questionable connections." Vince flashes through my mind.

"I don't follow."

"My dad…" I pause, gut churning, memories flashing through my mind like pictures in a photo album. "Married my mother, thinking she could… help him be better. But she couldn't, because he was already too far gone. And it cost her, *cost us*, everything."

"What happened, Danny?"

I hear the concern in her voice, the compassion, and I'm not sure I deserve it, but I *am* grateful for it. I lay my hand over hers and squeeze. "Where to start?" I say with a half-laugh. "The gambling addiction like grampy? The drugs, booze, and other women?" I spit out the words with disgust. "How he seduced my mother with promises of a golden future, then kept her in a loveless prison of a marriage until he beat her to a pulp one night and almost killed her?

She gasps. "Oh Danny. I'm so sorry."

"I was sixteen. I tried to step in, to save her. I woke up in the hospital with a broken arm and a concussion." I smile grimly. "I was the lucky one. When I woke up, I still had my brain function. My mom… wasn't so lucky." Only select few know this — that my mother basically became a ward of the State until I had amassed enough fortune to move her to full-time nursing care. "And where were the people my great-grandfather had helped, then?"

Nowhere. Except for Vince Fucking Ferrari. He helped me find a job, and checked in on me periodically. I may not like the asshole, but I do feel indebted to him.

"I went into foster care for two years and somehow managed to keep my nose clean. My high school math teacher saw something in me and encouraged me to apply to Stanford. I'm still not sure how it happened, but between my math scholarship, earning a walk-on spot on the crew team, and distilling whiskey, I made it work."

She lifts her head. "Wait. Say that again. You paid for college by distilling whiskey?"

I'm actually pretty proud of this. "I found Tom's whiskey formula in an old trunk of paraphernalia my mother showed me before she got hurt. On the back of a campaign poster was this formula. It wasn't too hard to figure out the process, and I made the first batch in the dorm. Harrison was my roommate, and he'd already pledged to Delta Chi, and once they'd tried my whiskey, they let me in too, so long as I kept them in spirits."

"The apple doesn't fall far from the tree."

"The bad apples don't seem to," I correct. "I never fit in with all those rich boys. I had to scrap and scrape for everything. They were using me for booze, but I was using them for information."

"A gangster to the core," she laughs.

"No," I correct. "That's smart business. Those rich guys? They're just as shady as the guys I knew on the East side. The only difference was they had the money, and with it, the power to make bad shit go away. I've made it my job to relieve them of their coin."

"So that you can help the vulnerable," she supplies. "Sounds an awful lot like another Robin Hood you mentioned."

I hate the comparison. But at the same time, helping people like Emmaline, like Lisa, and the others- it's the least I can do to balance the karma sheets.

"What ever happened to your dad?" she asks after a pause.

"He's in federal prison, serving year sixteen of a thirty-year sentence."

"Do you ever see him?"

I shake my head, the old anger and hurt flooding back. "The last time I saw him was the day he was sentenced. The judge asked me if I had anything to say. I stood, looked him straight in the eye, and told him I never wanted to see him again."

"Do you still feel that way?"

I nod, fisting the sheets. "After what he did to mom, to *us*. Dying's too good for him."

Roxi makes a sympathetic noise. "I know how that feels. Some people need to feel pain before they get to die." Her voice is hard. Brittle.

My curiosity is piqued, but before I can ask her what she meant by that, she slides her hand down my belly and inside my thighs. That's all it takes for a wave of arousal to ripple through me and wake up my cock. "Hungry again?" I tease.

"Mmm." She stretches beside me, pressing her body to mine, fingers tracing circles at the inside of my thighs until she cups my balls. "Famished." I'm fully erect now. Hard, and hungry myself, I lift my hips, intending to flip her onto her back, but she scoots out of reach with a giggle. "Not so fast, hot stuff. It's my turn to call the shots."

"Think so?" I challenge, half-hoping she sasses back. I'm not disappointed.

"Yep." She shoots me a predatory grin. "And you're gonna take it." She crawls over me and plants a kiss on my pec, then gives my nip a sharp little bite. The pain shoots like liquid lightning straight to my cock. I grunt with the pleasure of it.

"Think so?"

"Know so." She's blazing a trail with her tongue down my ribs and across my belly, sucking on the skin just below my navel, and it's hard as fuck to concentrate on her words, and not lose myself in the sensations ripping through me. My cock is heavy and long, bobbing a breath away from where her mouth is making tortuous patterns next to my hip bone. She looks up, eyes pools of liquid amber. I forget to breathe. Every cell in my body is holding its breath in anticipation of where her mouth is landing next. "You think you're so bad," she says, voice husky and dark. "But I know better. I see how you help people. People who desperately need someone on their side. But who takes care of you, Danny?"

No one. I swallow, trying to rid my throat of the lump that has somehow lodged itself there.

She makes a satisfied noise, as if confirming to herself what she knows to be true. "Just this once, you're going to let someone take care of you." Still holding my gaze, she licks my cock from root to crown. "Completely."

A shudder tears through me.

"Deny all you want," she says after licking me again. "But I know better. *I see you.*"

I'm cracked open. Half-crazed with desire and fear. It's like she reached through my chest and pulled out my still beating heart. "You know what happens to people who get too close to me," I rasp, on the verge of surrender. But I have to throw up some kind of last defense before she brings me to my knees. I have to at least try. "It never ends well," I warn. Surely, she's smart enough to connect the dots? She knows about Anita, about my mother, that's enough evidence to swear me off for good.

But it doesn't deter her, not in the least. Her eyes narrow like she already has my number, and there's no getting away from her. "They're not me." To prove her point, she takes me fully into her mouth, tongue sliding around the most sensitive part of me, applying just enough suction to send my eyes rolling into my head. My hips arch off the bed, my body silently begging for more. I let out a ragged sigh. "Roxi… you have no idea."

She answers with a throaty moan that vibrates down the length of me, melting my brain. I swear she's smiling like a goddamned Cheshire Cat while she sucks me off, humming and making all manner of delighted noises. Her hands are everywhere her mouth isn't — scraping her fingernails along the inside of my thighs, cupping my balls, pulling on the skin behind them, stroking the part of my cock that won't fit into her mouth. It's too much, my brain goes on overload as a chain reaction is set off in my body, starting at the base of my spine and spiraling outward like an exploding star. I'm covered in sweat, muscles straining, and when the shockwave reaches my head, I nearly pass out from the light bursting behind my eyes. I come with a shout, emptying myself into her mouth, clutching at her hair, scrabbling for some kind of purchase as my insides are ripped out and all that remains of who I was is a shell, a husk. My eyes prickle. I can't let myself believe she nearly brought me to tears, because I've vowed to never let any woman have that much power over me. I blink back the wetness once. Then again.

I caress her bright copper waves as she licks every drop

of come from me, then returns to curl into the hollow of my arm. She drops her head to my chest with what can only be described as a self-satisfied sigh of pure contentment. I press a kiss to her head, marveling at the wonder of her. "Thank you," I murmur.

I lay awake watching as her eyes flutter shut and sleep claims her, unable to shake the feeling that men like me are never this lucky. At least not for long.

Chapter Fourteen

We arrive back in Kansas City two days later, and the closer we get to home, the worse I feel. This weekend was... perfect. Otherworldly. Someone more romantic would call it a fairytale. Whatever it was, it wasn't reality, and what happens in Napa, stays in Napa. Which means, Roxi and I must return to stolen glances, the occasional kiss for show, and long nights of frustrated sleep. How do we cross back over a line we busted through with weapons of mass destruction?

Roxi is unusually silent. I assume that she's consumed with similar thoughts, but at the moment, I'm too much of a coward to ask. I glance her direction as I pull the Lotus out of the parking lot at the downtown airport. "Fuck it," I growl as we roll to a stop at the light at Broadway and 35. "I'm not ready for this to end." I look over to her. "Can I take you to dinner?"

Her eyes warm and crinkle as that big beautiful smile spreads across her face. "I'd love that. Where to?"

I switch lanes, and take a left after the overpass, then wind us through the River Market to a little French restaurant I like in Columbus Park. It's quiet and out of the way, and Roxi's gonna love the food. "Just a little place I know."

In minutes, I'm pulling into another parking space and rounding the car to open her door.

"We're eating here?" she says excitedly as she reads the small sign saying Le Fou Frog. "I've always wanted to try this place."

"You've lived here how long, and you haven't?" I tease.

She shrugs. "I always thought it was a place for a special occasion or a fancy date."

"But you must have dated before?" She's obviously no virgin, though my chest puffs at the thought there's been no one special previously. That there are still places in Kansas City she's yet to discover. And more importantly, that I can share them with her.

She rolls her eyes. "Yes. But you might have noticed I'm a bit of a workaholic."

"But all work and no play…"

"Makes me horny and frustrated."

I let go with a belly laugh and pull her close, dropping a kiss on that filthy mouth. "Good thing I know how to take care of that."

Marcel, the owner, greets us personally. "Danny, so good to see you," he says with a thick French accent. "Eet has been too long. And who is zis beautiful sing?"

"Roxi, meet Marcel."

He pulls her in for kisses on both cheeks. "Enchanter, Madame. Bienvenue." He turns to me. "And where have you been keeping zis beauty?" he asks with a droll wink.

"All to myself," I answer with a wink back, which earns me an elbow to the ribs from Roxi.

"Ah. I see," he says with a knowing smile. "So zee best table for you, ce soir. Follow me." He leads us to a dimly lit corner table for two. "Stay as long as you like. I will bring zee wine as soon as you are ready."

Roxi clears her throat, eyes twinkling. "I think we're ready right now." When Marcel has departed, she turns to me. "How did you find this place?"

"Vince Ferrari helped me get a job here bussing tables when I was sixteen — right after my dad... well you know. Marcel took me under his wing, made sure I stayed out of trouble."

She cocks her head. "*Vince* helped you?"

I nod, unsure of what to make of her reaction. "Believe me, I'm not his biggest fan. But he helped me when I had no one to turn to."

"Does he hold it over you? That he helped you?"

"No. He was one of the first members when I opened the Whiskey Den."

"He's never asked you for favors?"

"Just to set up poker games, but that's a benefit I extend to all my members. Why the quizzing?"

Her face freezes for a split second. "Just curious," she says, flashing me a sheepish smile. "I led a more... sheltered life. All I was allowed to do to stay out of trouble was math camp."

I snort. "I bet you never got into trouble. I bet you were a good girl, weren't you?"

"Who me?" She feigns an innocent look. "It's amazing what you can get away with when people peg you for the good girl."

I lean forward, dropping a hand to her thigh. "Admit it. You've been dirty since the get-go, haven't you?"

She straightens in her seat. "A lady never kisses and tells," she says primly, drawing another laugh from me.

I don't recognize myself, this person who's relaxed. Enjoying the company of a lovely woman, and not contemplating his next move, or three moves out. Not worrying about douchebags and whose ass I'm going to have to kick next, or what vulnerable person is going to need my help next. "If it meant I'd do every naughty thing to you that you asked for tonight, would you tell?"

She gives me a calculating stare, eyes growing hotter with each passing second. "Mmm, tempting."

I slide my hand higher. "Is this tempting enough for you?"

She squirms a little in her seat and flicks her eyebrows. "Okay, I'll play. But you go first."

"Ask me anything."

The words leave her mouth instantly. "Virginity."

I grin. "Summer I was fifteen, Peter Conklin's basement with his older sister who was nineteen."

She purses her lips, but her eyes are sparkling. "Ooh, so naughty."

"You?"

She pauses. "Twenty. Sophomore year. I thought I was in love."

I can't resist pushing. "Did he give you an orgasm?"

She snorts. "What do you think? Every college girl knows there are toys for that."

I shake my head with a tsk. "I would have given you one."

"Did your nineteen-year-old fuck buddy tell you how to find her clitoris? Because if not, I'm guessing it took a few tries to, er... work your magic," she says with a smirk.

Marcel interrupts us long enough to drop a bottle of Bordeaux and fill our glasses. As soon as he's out of earshot, I pepper her with questions. "When did you have your first orgasm?"

"With another person? Because I'm pretty sure I

figured out how to give myself one when I was six years old."

I choke on my wine.

"Don't act so surprised. I'm sure you were pulling on your penis when you were that age."

I'm sure I was too, but I don't remember it. "Okay, so with someone, then."

"Early twenties? I don't remember the date, but I remember the man. I dated a PhD candidate my junior year who… umm… taught me a lot."

"Including that you like spanky public shit," I fill in for her.

She blushes furiously and nods. "I wasn't ready to settle down, and he was looking for a wife, so I broke his heart. But, I *am* grateful."

"Roxi Rickoli, heart breaker."

She smirks. "It's possible I've left a string of broken men in my wake."

"Roxi Rickoli, egomaniac," I add, squeezing the inside of her thigh. I change the subject. "Why the snake tattoo?"

She looks away and takes a slow sip of her wine. "How old were you when you got your pec tatt?"

"I got it after Anita died."

She nods as if she understands, and the air between us changes from playful to serious. "I have a sister. *Had* a sister," she corrects.

Tension radiates off her, and all my senses go on high alert.

"I… worshipped her," she says, voice thick with emotion. "She was smart, funny, loving… and a total ass-kicker." She pauses and takes another slow sip of her wine and starts to trace circles on the tablecloth. My stomach flops. She's talking in the past tense. Instinctively, I shift closer to her.

Her mouth tilts up. "She made me feel like I could conquer the world, that I could be anything, accomplish anything. Looking back, I can see she was a raging feminist, an activist. And I'm proud that some of her passion rubbed off on me."

"What happened? How did you lose her?"

She shuts her eyes, as if drawing up courage, strength to speak. "She was murdered. Brutally." She speaks in a monotone. It's not the first time she's told the story, but I know from experience the telling of shit never gets easier, so I don't press her for details, even though my curiosity is piqued.

"Did they find him?" I ask, voice dropping to basement levels. "Whoever he is, I hope he's suffering. Mightily."

She shakes her head. "Her case is still unsolved."

Her words are like a punch to the gut.

"So the tattoo… I remember her telling me about a women's studies class she'd taken on ancient matriarchal cultures and how snakes were a sign of feminine power and healing, and how patriarchal cultures subverted that." She sniffs, then sighs. "So on my eighteenth birthday, I went to the local tattoo artist with a design." She shakes her head with a wry grin. "My father was furious."

"So this," I trace her leg where I've memorized the pattern. "Is a tribute to your sister."

She nods. "Yeah. And a reminder of my own strength."

My chest pulls so tight it's hard to breathe. I reach for her hand and bring it to my lips. "You're remarkable, Roxi."

We linger over dinner, neither of us making a move to wind it up. Marcel has kindly given us space, but I can see he's pacing by the hostess stand. I tilt my head his direction. "I think he's ready for us to leave."

Roxi looks over and nods in agreement. "I think you're right." She covers my hand with hers. "I… thank you for tonight. This has been lovely. I wasn't ready to go home either."

Something about the tone of her voice digs at me, gives me a little push. "What about now?"

She hesitates, and her silence speaks volumes. My chest feels heavy and tight again. *What happens in Napa stays in Napa.* "I don't know how to put the genie back in the box," she confesses. "I don't know how to go back to the way things were."

"Who says we have to?"

She gives me a crooked smile. "I *am* your employee."

"I could fire you. I'm sure another company would snap you up in a heartbeat." But I hate that idea with a passion. I don't want her spending her days someplace else, so she can spend her nights with me. I'm a selfish bastard, and I fucking want it all.

She makes a face of pure disgust. "Eww. No."

"So are you admitting you like working for me?"

"As far as bosses go, you're pretty good."

I lean in, pulling her hair from her neck so I can nuzzle the sensitive spot underneath her ear. "You just like the benefits," I tease. My voice drops. "Come home with me."

Chapter Fifteen

I fidget with my key fob all the way up the elevator. I've never brought a woman into my domain before — at least not with the intention of having her spend the night — and my brain runs through a mental checklist. What does she like for breakfast? Does she even eat breakfast? Coffee or tea? Or juice?

But as soon as the elevator opens, and we've entered my space, my worries fly away. She gasps, covering her mouth as she takes it all in — the open concept kitchen, the leather couches, the floor to ceiling windows that look north to Downtown. "This view, Danny. Wow."

I shoot her a grin while giving a silent fist pump. "I'm glad you like it."

She bends and gives me a view of her luscious ass. It takes me a second to realize she's removing her weapon. "Do you have a safe?"

"No, but I can have one sent over first thing."

"Is there somewhere safe you'd like me to stow this?"

Fuck, I don't know. But after her confession at dinner, I can understand why she's so focused on personal protection. "How about inside the credenza by the front door?" She hands it over and even though I return a moment later, the living room's empty. "Roxi?"

"In here," she calls from my bedroom.

I enter my room to discover her splayed across the bed wearing nothing but her bra and very see through panties. The hard-on that comes is pretty instantaneous, although it's been building in fits and starts all evening. The Fou Frog was like one continuous foreplay, and now I'm ready for the main event.

I pull my shirt from my slacks, and take my time unbuttoning, reveling in the way her eyes rove hungrily over my body. Especially when I shrug out of my shirt and toss it over a low ottoman. I make sure to flex with each movement so that I'm giving her a little show. I pause with my hand on my belt, loving how she bites her lip as she's watching, anticipating. She flicks her gaze up, and our gazes tangle. The heat between us rises an easy ten degrees. "Take it off, already," she bosses, voice husky and eager.

"It's going to cost you," I say, because I can't resist drawing this out as long as possible.

"Oh?"

"Yep."

"And what exactly, is it going to cost?"

I tap a finger to my lips, thinking. "So many choices," I murmur.

She pushes herself up to half-sitting. "How about I make this easier for you?" She reaches behind her back and makes short work of the clasps. But she doesn't reveal the plush, sensuous flesh beneath.

"Tease," I rasp. Her delighted smirk pulls a laugh from me. She drops first one strap, then the other, so that her lacy undergarment is now resting on her tight, hard nipples. My cock jerks. I whip off my belt, and push out of my slacks and bottoms in one move, freeing my cock. It juts between us, heavy and hard, precome beading at the tip.

"Come here," she practically growls, eyes riveted on my swollen cock.

I close the distance in two steps and hook a finger at the center of her bra and yank, freeing her peachy rose colored tips. My mouth waters to taste her. We reach for each other, her hand coming to my cock, mine to a breast so I can brush a thumb across the sensitive tip. We sink to the bed and end up facing away from each other. I have half a mind to flip her around, but then her mouth lands on my cock, tongue circling my crown then sliding down to my root, while her hand plays with my balls.

Bring it.

She props up her leg, presenting her pussy, and who'm I to say no to a feast? I nip at the inside of her thigh then slide my tongue through her slick folds, going straight for her clit. Everything I do with my mouth, she mimics on my cock, and we take turns teasing each other until we're both panting and squirming. The sensation of licking while being licked is a mind fuck, but one so good, I want more. "If I had lube, I'd have my finger up your pretty little rosebud of an ass," I say, nearly coming when she groans around my cock. I take another hit of her pussy, filling my senses with her taste, her scent, until I can hardly stand it. I pull away long enough to order her to move. "On your hands and knees." She complies with an eager noise in her throat, and I rise to my knees, sliding the head of my cock through her swollen pussy lips. I tease her until she's thrusting back, seeking relief.

I bend over her, wrapping an arm around her soft belly, and drive into her. The sound of my balls slapping against her only serves to drive both of us to new heights. She meets each thrust with one of her own, adding a little twist and a wriggle at the end that makes me crazy. I slide my palm down over her trimmed mound to cup her sex, seeking and finding her clit, sliding over it with each thrust, giving her the slow, steady rhythm I know she likes. She drops her head with a deep groan. "*Oh Danny*. It's so deep. I think I'm going to break."

"No sweetheart, you're going to fly," I murmur. "Let go. I've got you." I bend, covering her completely, and bite her shoulder, while I find her nipples with my other hand and give a firm pinch. That's what sends her over the edge, and I pinch again, harder, as I drive into her, eyes losing focus as she comes so hard on my cock, that for a second, I forget to breathe. And then I'm exploding, spilling my seed deep in her cunt, vision narrowing, as wave after wave of release crashes over me. She drops to her elbows and bows her head, breath coming in harsh gasps. She wriggles and moans, and I drive into her again, taking my cues from her. "Do you want more, sweetheart?"

She answers with a nod and a grunt, and I continue to stroke into her and slide my fingers back and forth over the sensitized bundle of nerves until she cries out and shatters a second time. We collapse to our sides, and I pull her flush against my chest. We stay that way, spent, as our brains slowly return to our bodies. And in that moment, I recognize two things. First, I will never be the same again. Roxi has ruined me for all others. Second, that I am utterly and totally in love. And I have no idea how to tell her.

Chapter Sixteen

I wake up to an empty bed, and the sound of the Beatles coming from the kitchen. I throw on a pair of sweats and make my way down the hall and stop short at the picture in front of me. Roxi's appropriated my flannel robe, and is stirring at the stove, hair piled on top of her head in a messy bun. But what captivates me, what makes me fall more in love with her, is the off-key singing of Penny Lane as she dumps half a bag of shredded cheese into the pan.

I lean on the wall and watch, a stupid grin plastered on my face. She's bobbing in time with the music, shimmying her hips as she stirs. I commit this picture of her to memory. Waking up with her in my bed every day for the last two-and-a half weeks have been... incredible. I've learned she's not a morning person but she loves morning sex, that she loves her coffee with so much cream it's tan, and she still insists on driving herself to work — *"Because I'm staying over, not moving in."*

At first it was just her suitcase. But then it was an extra pair of shoes, and a few extra undergarments. Now she has her own dresser drawer, and her preferred bottle of shampoo in the shower. She may still be housesitting, but in my mind, she's living here.

And I like it.

A lot.

I can't resist not touching her any longer, so I make my presence known, and slip behind her, wrapping my arms around her waist and nuzzling her neck. "Mmm. Cheesy eggs? How'd you know they're my favorite?"

Her laugh is sweet and husky as she leans back into me, still swaying with the music. "My super-psychic spidey powers."

"You didn't have to get up and cook. I'd have made something."

She turns off the burner, then swivels to face me, looping her arms around my neck and giving me a kiss. She tastes like orange juice. "I know. But I wanted to do something special for you this morning. Today's the day you usually visit your mom, right?"

So. Fucking. Observant. My heart swells. Visiting mom is... depressing. And even though she's only been here a short time, she's already keyed into my emotions, as much as I try and play those cards close. Maybe it's because her act of kindness has caught me off guard, but the words slip out as if I was used to saying them every day. "I love you, Rox."

She pulls back, eyes searching mine, then flashes me one of her signature wide smiles. "Yeah? You sure you're not just bamboozled by my fabulous tits?"

Leave it to her to make light of my declaration. But I'm not letting it go. Not this time. "Oh, I'm absofucking-lutely dazzled by your fabulous tits, and the way you are in bed, and your off-key singing, and your very sexy tattoo." My voice turns to gravel as I fight to find the words. "And your passion, and how you squeeze the toothpaste from the bottom and wash out the cap. I'm ensorceled, and I've fallen for you hook, line, and sinker." My pulse races, and my chest grows tight as I watch her for any inkling of a reaction.

Her face softens, and she grazes my cheek with the back of her knuckles. "And I love you too, Danny. You can keep trying to convince me you're a big, bad wolf, but I know better." She hesitates, biting her lip. "And no matter what happens in the future, I want you to know — right now — that I'm crazy about you," she adds, kissing the corner of my mouth.

I lift her to the counter and slip my hands underneath the robe, sliding my palms up her thighs. Maybe it's because I'm giddy from our mutual declarations, high on endorphins instead of caffeine, but my senses are heightened. Her skin feels silkier under my palms. The fuzz of the flannel, softer. The scent of her, more heavenly, the taste of her when we kiss, better.

And kiss we do. By the time we pull apart, my morning wood is tenting my sweats. She eyes my bulge with a sly smile. "Hungry for more than breakfast?"

"Always." I slide my hands higher up her thighs, caressing her sex, as wet as I am hard. "It seems I'm not the only one."

She opens her legs a little wider and I part her folds, sliding one, then two fingers into her sweet heat. "I want your cock, not your fingers," she urges, hands pushing down my waistband. I love that sometimes with her, it's fucking full-stop. The counter is at the perfect height and she wraps her legs around me as I slide into her with a sigh of relief. She yanks open her robe, pressing her tits against my chest, and dropping her head to leave a bite on my shoulder. "Yes," she says through gritted teeth as I thrust into her, burying myself in her hot pussy. "I love this, love you deep inside me, pushing hard."

"I love your hot little cunt," I grunt. "The way you squeeze me. So… tight."

I can sense her winding up. Her breaths come faster, sharper, the tiny noises of enjoyment she makes in the back of her throat, deeper. And I'm right there with her, ready to spill myself into the deepest part of her. Her fingernails dig into my back and it eggs me on, I push harder, deeper, as deep as I can go, focusing on my breathing to hold the inevitable at bay until she drops her head with a cry, and this morning, a laugh, as she shudders in my arms, and I let go, spilling my come into her hot, tight, pussy. "God, I fucking love you," I roar as a laugh rumbles out of me and mingles with hers.

Visions of babies and forever dance behind my eyes, and for once, I don't banish them. But I do keep them to myself, at least for now. She side-eyes the eggs. "I think they're still warm," she says with a rueful smile. I grab a fork and scoop some up, feeding her a bite. "Mmm. Yummers," she says, shutting her eyes.

I follow up with a bite, myself. There are bits of bacon cooked into the eggy, cheesy goo, and it's delicious. "Where'd you learn to cook like this?"

"My dad used to make this special breakfast for us when we were kids — cheesy bacon and eggs. I always thought he should market it."

"Come with me today," I blurt. "Come meet my mom."

"Of course," she answers with genuine warmth. "I'm happy to come anytime, but don't feel like you have to… now that we're…" she waves between us.

I capture both her hands, holding both of them still.

"I've never introduced anyone... significant to my mom." I let the words hang between us.

Her eyes warm. "So I'm... *significant*, huh?" She reaches for another bite of egg, this time feeding it to me.

I decide to lay all the cards on the table. "You're it for me, babe. I might have loved Anita the way a dumb twenty-year-old loves, but no one's come close to the way I feel about you. And even though she won't understand it, or remember the conversation, I want my mom to meet the woman I love."

Roxi beams. "Aww, see? You *are* a big ole teddy bear." She tilts her chin, indicating she expects a kiss, which I happily give her.

"Nope. I'm not," I argue. "But... you *do* make me want to be a better man. The best kind of man." I just hope it's enough for her.

Chapter Seventeen

"*S*o I have an idea."

Roxi turns from polishing glasses behind the bar. "Lay it on me, teddy bear." She's taken to calling me that ever since I took her to visit my mom. Only in private, but I keep waiting for her to drop the name in front of Harrison or Stockton, just for laughs.

"I'd like the Whiskey Den to host a Thanksgiving buffet in the parking lot."

Her eyebrows shoot skyward. "On Thanksgiving?"

I nod. "My great-grandfather used to host an enormous Thanksgiving here in the West Bottoms, free to anyone. It was part of what made him super popular. I think I'd like to resurrect the tradition."

Her brows knit together. "Why? Are you thinking of running for office?"

I shake my head with a laugh. "No. I just thought it'd be a nice way to give back. That's all."

She rounds the bar and slips between my legs, looping her arms around my neck. "I think it's a wonderful idea. Teddy bear," she adds with a smirk, before kissing me.

It's early afternoon and it's slow. I have half a mind to take her back to the stockroom for a little sneaky time. But Vince's voice behind us pours cold water on that thought.

"Can I talk to you?" he asks gruffly, not bothering with pleasantries.

"I've got to pull inventory," Roxi says, disengaging from my embrace and hurrying back to the stockroom. With any other client, I'd have told her to stay, but not with the way Vince keeps eyeing her when he thinks I'm not watching.

"What can I do for you, Vince?"

"I'd like to set up another poker game."

"Sure thing. When?"

"Tonight."

I bite back an exasperated sigh. Lately, I've gotten the feeling that Vince has been purposefully testing my limits. But so far, he hasn't violated any of the Whiskey Den membership rules, and I'm not about to boot him just because I think he's an asshole. "It depends on your players. How many do I need to vet?"

"Only one." He hands me a piece of paper with a name on it. *Alex Descharmes.* I study his bold scrawl, racking my brain as to why I know that name. It'll come to me, it always does. And my vetting process is thorough, so I'm sure I'll figure out why that name means something to me. I nod once. "I'll give you a call by five. Do you want me to fill the other spots?"

He nods.

"Anything else? Can I pour you something?"

"Not today. I have an… appointment. See you this evening?"

"I'll be here." *Watching your ass.* I raise my hand as he leaves the bar. As soon as the door closes behind him, I pull out my phone and call Harrison.

"'Sup?" he asks by way of greeting.

"You busy tonight?"

"Poker game?"

"Yep."

"I gotta pass tonight."

"Why?" I scoff. "Hot date?"

"Yeah. With the gym." He doesn't sound pleased.

"Blow it off."

"No can do."

"Your loss. Can you let Stockton know?"

"He'll be there. Who else is on the list?"

"Vince, some new guy I've got to vet — Alex Descharmes? Does that name ring a bell?"

"Can't help you there. Who else?"

"I still have to make calls, but the usual suspects — Dmitri and Robert Templeton. Any suggestions in case I need a fifth?"

"Actually, yeah. First baseman for the Kings — Robbie Moran. He's got more money than Christ, and an attitude to go with it. I'd love him to be relieved of some of it."

"Will you make the call?"

"You bet. Catch up with you soon?"

"You know where to find me." I stuff my phone in my pocket and head back to my office to grab my laptop. I poke my head in the stockroom "You can come out now." But it's empty. "Roxi?" She probably stepped into the restaurant that shares a back wall with the Den, but I can't help the niggle of worry that ripples through me. I head down to the office, and bump smack into her *as she's shutting the door.* She squeals in surprise as I catch her. "What the fuck are you doing in there?" I growl.

For the first time ever in our relationship, she looks scared. "I-I'm sorry. I was just stowing my gun."

I narrow my eyes, suspicion burning a hole in my belly.

Maybe it's leftover from Vince, but something feels terribly, horribly off. "How'd you get in? The door's always locked and I have the only key."

"I-it was open a crack. I thought it would be okay. I didn't touch anything, I swear."

I hate this. She knows my office is off-limits, and that it's for her own safety. She knows I keep my laptop password protected and under lock and key. It's for her protection as much as mine. "Why were you in there, Roxi?"

"I told you," she snaps. "I was stowing my weapon. Just like you require."

I don't like that we're arguing. I don't like that this brings up all my old suspicions of her. I don't like it at all. I also don't have time to deal with it right now. I've got to run a series of deep checks on this Alex character. As it is, I'm going to be pushing right up against my five o'clock deadline to pull together a game. "I'm sorry I snapped, but you know I can't have you in there."

"Why? Because I'm going to hack your computer?" she says in a voice heavy with sarcasm. "This is about Vince, isn't it?"she demands. "He's trying to set up another game."

I nod. "It's for everyone's protection."

She crosses her arms. "When are you going to give them up?"

"The poker games? Never." I'd be a fool to give them up. The money is too easy.

"But you don't need the money."

I let out a dry laugh. "I *always* need the money, sweetheart." She more than anyone should understand that, given my financial responsibilities.

She glares. "How is this being a *better man*? She uses air quotes throwing my words back at me.

"This is business," I grit. "Those guys are going to play

anyway. So why not here? Where people know I enforce strict rules of conduct, and that I'll expose their shit if they fuck with me."

"Nice," she sneers. "That whole honor among thieves goes a long way to making you a better man."

"This game has nothing to do with us."

"Doesn't it?" She gives me a look that says she completely disagrees.

Heat races up my neck. "I'm not gonna justify myself to you or anyone else, sweetheart. If you don't like it, you're welcome to the door."

"So you'd just kick me out?"

"Not out of my life, but if you don't like the way I practice business, you're welcome to work elsewhere." I don't like that choice, but she needs to understand that just because she shares my bed, she does not share my business.

"And what if you get caught?" Her voice catches. "Then what?"

"It's a closed circle. No way I'm going to get caught. Now, if you'll excuse me, I have work to do, and you have glasses to polish." I hate putting her in her place like that, and I know there will be fallout later tonight once we get home, but we can talk about it then. I brush past her and shut the door behind me and turn the lock.

I walk straight to my desk and pull out the drawer where I keep her weapon. Sure enough, it's there. I double check my laptop, and it looks untouched. I'm probably just being paranoid, I tell myself. Vince has me spooked. But as I pull open my laptop, instead of entering the information on Alex Descharmes, I start searching for articles related to Roxi's sister. But it's like looking for a needle in a haystack.

I've refrained from searching thus far, wanting to give Roxi the benefit of the doubt, and I know how hard it is to talk about details relating to the tragedy of someone you love. But now? I'm driven to find out. I need to reassure myself that Roxi's legit, that she hasn't been playing me. I assume she's close to my age, and all I know for sure was that she was college-age, and killed before Roxi turned eighteen. I enter a five-year search window… and come up empty handed. Although, I'm shocked at the number of unsolved murders still out there, and disgusted that most of them are female victims. Some are easy to rule out. Two where the bodies haven't been found, one is African-American, another was an exchange student. I keep coming back to three of them — I grimace as I read through graphic details of these young women's last moments, the memory of my mother's screams of terror as fresh in my mind as if it were yesterday.

As I read the articles, clenching my fist and entertaining fantasies of vigilante revenge a la the Green Arrow, my chest fills with lead. Not only do none of the women look remotely like Roxi, none of them share any common details with the few details of her life she's shared with me. My gut clenches. She can't be lying. I refuse to believe it. She's too genuine, and brutally honest when it comes to her feelings. I'm the one that hides shit, not her.

I decide on the spot that I'm going to ask her about this after the game tonight. I need to give her the opportunity to explain herself before I jump to conclusions. But I can't help but wonder if I've been blinded by our chemistry, and if I have been, what next?

Chapter Eighteen

*W*e give each other a wide berth the rest of the afternoon, which I also hate. Although I suppose it's normal for couples to have disagreements. Hell, Anita and I shouted at each other weekly. Sometimes more.

Stockton strolls into the Den a little after nine-thirty, top button on his shirt open, tie loose. "You look like you've had a day."

He scowls. "Yeah, you could say that."

"What's your poison tonight?"

"Something that will make me forget I woke up this morning."

I wince. "That bad, huh?" I signal Roxi, who meets us by one of the wingbacks Stockton has sunk into. "Can you bring Stockton a tumbler of Pappy Van Winkle, no ice? Top shelf, far left."

Her eyes flick between me and Stockton, and she nods once, and retreats to the bar without saying a word.

"Trouble in paradise?" Stockton asks.

"Nothing that won't be fixed later with a little booze, a little talk—"

"And a lot of fucking," Stockton supplies.

If only it were that easy. Roxi drops the drinks, keeping her eyes averted. I feel like there's a knife lodged in my sternum, and it twists every time she looks away, or refuses to make eye-contact. Worst of all, I can tell I've upset her. Her easygoing smile that naturally draws everyone into her orbit is missing. Tonight, her mouth is pinched, and the corners are pulled down. Her eyes have lost their amused sparkle and she seems... resigned. I cast a glance in Stockton's direction. He's a million miles away, contemplating the amber liquid in his glass. "I'll be right back." He barely acknowledges me.

I make a beeline for the bar, and as soon as Roxi's finished serving number sixty-four, a pro-basketball player from L. A., I wave a hand, grabbing her attention. I motion to the stockroom, and head there to wait. She follows shortly after. The look in her eye is unsettling. It's a side of her I've never seen — determined, angry... worried. I take her into my arms. "Hey."

"Hey." She stays stiff.

Warning bells sound in my head. "Look, I'm sorry I snapped at you earlier. I behaved... badly." It takes a lot for me to admit that, because I feel like I'm the one who was wronged. But I can also see that I was a dick. I didn't need to pull rank, and trot out accusations based on fear and not facts. She nods, which I guess means she's accepted my apology. "We should talk tonight, after the poker game. You know, clear the air. But, I wanted you to know that everything's okay. And if there's something we need to address, let's talk about it."

She looks like she's ready to burst into tears. "Roxi, sweetheart? What is it? Do you need to go home? I can take over and close up the front when it's time for the poker game."

She shakes her head vehemently. "I… I'm fine. I'm just, it's just… I know people have disagreements, but this afternoon rattled me. I'll be okay." She forces a smile, and the knife in my chest twists hard, because she's lying. She's not fine, and I hate that she doesn't trust me, trust *us*, enough to be honest with her feelings.

I smooth her hair from her face. "Look, whatever it is. We'll figure it out, together, okay? I'm not going anywhere." I drop a kiss on her temple. Her body vibrates with tension, but when I kiss her again, a shudder ripples through her and she lets out a heavy sigh. She nods, shoulders relaxing slightly. I'll consider that a win and make a mental note to stop by our favorite late-night burger joint for the Big Whammy — bacon cheeseburger, fries, and a shake. Once we've had food, and a little naughty time, like Stockton suggested, we'll be back to ourselves.

I follow Roxi out to the bar and help myself to a half-glass of the Pappy Van Winkle, and return to Stockton, dropping into the chair next to him. His glass is half-finished, and he's looking slightly revived. He leans forward and speaks in a low voice. "I've been meaning to ask you something," he starts.

"Shoot."

"I think Dmitri and Vince are exchanging more than just money at the poker table."

I don't believe that for a second. With as much dirt as I have stashed away on the two of them, there's no way they'd break the rules. But I'll hear out Stockton, even if his ideas are completely far-fetched, bordering on paranoid. "What makes you think that?"

"Just a… a feeling."

I scoff. "I don't deal in feelings. It's not my problem

how you all decide to pay each other after the games. You know the rules."

Stockton glares at me. "It is if they're dealing in humans."

Now he's got my attention. He's usually pretty mild-mannered, so the fact he's shooting daggers at me and tightening his grip on his glass is significant. But still, I can't believe Vince and Dmitri would risk their membership at the Den by breaking the rules. They saw what I did to Ivo. In spite of all that, I bite. "What makes you think it's humans?" I swear, if they've been trafficking under my nose, I will cut them into tiny pieces and feed them to the fish in river. I'm a Pendergast for fuck's sake, and I may not be proud of my family's history, but I will not hesitate to bring down an asshole by any means necessary.

Stockton glances around and leans closer. "Last poker night, when you left the room to grab drinks, I overheard Dmitri telling Vince he'd pay him in *real-estate.*" He air-quotes real-estate.

My mouth twitches, and I double check the liquor in his glass. "Did you start drinking before you got here?

Stockton's face darkens. "Fuck no."

I can't help the grin that pulls at my mouth. "You *do* know Dmitri's a real-estate mogul, and Vince, among other things, develops properties. Why wouldn't Dmitri pay him in real-estate?"

Stockton is clearly not satisfied. "I don't know, man. Something about the whole exchange sounded off. I swear they were talking about people, not buildings or land."

"Feelings are not facts. Bring me proof. Until then, you know the Whiskey Den motto — see no evil, hear no evil. That motto has saved your ass on a number of occasions," I remind him after taking a sip.

But Stockton's like a fucking terrier when he gets an

idea in his head, and he won't let this go. "You know you're like a brother to me, man. But I think that's a crap motto. And someday, it's going to catch up with you. And I don't want to be the one to bail you out of jail when it does."

I flash Stockton a smile. "Someday doesn't come if you always do things by the books and follow all the rules. You were the one who taught me that."

"But your rules aren't everyone else's rules," Stockton points out. "And that's why I'm worried."

Chapter Nineteen

I want a do-over. I want to wake up next to Roxi at the beginning of this day and do things differently. I want to not argue with Roxi, and I want to not give Stockton top-shelf whiskey when he's clearly upset about something.

But in spite of my bravado, Stockton's accusations have rattled me. If Vince and Dmitri are dealing in humans, I fucking want to know about it, because I will shut that shit down. I will boot them from the club so fast they won't realize their kidneys are up by their throats, thanks to the kick up the ass I've given them.

There's nothing to do but wait. I indulge in another half-tumbler of Pappy Van Winkle with Stockton. I typically refuse to drink at all on poker nights, but it's been a rough day, and I've only had the equivalent of one glass over two hours. I'm plenty alert for any funny business.

Promptly at eleven, Vince, Dmitri, and their associate Alex walk in. I welcome them and send them to the bar for their first round. A few minutes later Robert Templeton joins us. "Since we're all here, why don't we get started early?" I offer. The earlier we start, the earlier we'll be done, and the sooner Roxi and I can head home and commence making-up. I follow the men to the back room, and begin to set up the cards, like I always do, while the men make small-talk.

Just as the men begin to make their way to the back room, Oscar waves me to the door. "This guy, Moran, says he's here for a meeting?"

Meeting is our code word for the game for anyone who's not a member. "Moran?" It hits me, and I slap my forehead. "Fuck. Yeah. Let him in. Harrison made the call. He's good." Motherfucker. Yet another piece in today's shit show. It's happened before, and it's not the end of the world, but it's just one more reason I want this day to fucking end.

"It's Robbie, right?" I extend my hand.

He nods, eyes scanning the room. "Harrison said Stockton would be here?"

I nod. "He's already in back. Follow me."

I enter the room and take my place at the far wall, just like I always do. "Gentleman, meet Robbie Moran, he'll be joining us tonight."

Vince scowls. "Who's he? I set up this game and I sure as fuck didn't invite him."

"His money's as good as yours, Vince. You have a problem?" My voice takes on a hard edge. I will *not* have Vincent fucking with me. Not tonight.

"Yeah. I didn't invite him."

"Well, I did, and it's my house, my rules. Questions?" Vince looks like he wants to say a lot more, but he wisely keeps his mouth shut. I re-explain the buy in and the rules, and begin to shuffle.

Tonight, Alex sits to my left, Dmitri to my right. Next to Dmitri is Vince, Moran is next to Vince, and Templeton sits on the other side of the door next to Stockton. The first round is uneventful. Vince and Robbie duke it out until Robbie folds. It's obvious this isn't Robbie's first game, and I make a mental note to ask Harrison more about him at a later date. He might be a good candidate to be Ivo's replacement. Membership offers are not made lightly, and when a member leaves — for whatever reason, any replacement is thoroughly vetted, financially and personally.

I text Roxi to bring in a round of drinks. Normally, with this crew, I have no problem stepping out to grab drinks. But tonight, just like this entire day, feels off, and I don't feel like giving Vince the benefit of the doubt, especially after what Stockton mentioned. Roxi comes in after I've dealt the first two cards, and the game is temporarily paused while she asks for drink orders. I hardly pay attention until I see Vince leering at her out of the corner of my eye. Literally salivating while he's staring at her tits.

I've fucking had it. "Eyes on your cards, Ferrari," I snap.

As if in slow motion, Vince's head swivels my direction. His lip curls. "And what if I don't?"

I spread my arms, and speak as evenly as I can, given that I want to rip this motherfucker's face off. "My house, my rules. If you can't keep your eyes on your cards, I'll ban your ass."

"I don't think you want to do that," Vince says with a hint of a threat in his voice.

"And I don't think you want to threaten me." The room goes still, and the other players exchange glances.

Vince's eyes narrow to glittering points. I can see now, why people are afraid of him. But I'm not. I faced down meaner as a sixteen-year-old in my first knife fight, Vince can't touch me. "Ban me, and I'll make sure my associates ruin you."

Stockton throws down his cards. "Like hell you will."

I rise and turn on Stockton. "You. Sit. This is my fight." I turn back to Vince. "The only reason I'm not kicking your ass out now is that I don't need the headache of returning funds from an interrupted game. Threaten me again and you're out. *Capisci?*" I'm dead calm. If he tried to start a fight right now, I'd have no problem snapping his neck.

Roxi re-enters with a tray full of drinks, takes one look and stops, worry on her face. "Everything okay, gentlemen? I can come back."

In the next instant, all hell breaks loose. A black figure appears at the door with a rifle. "FBI, everyone on the floor." As that happens, all six men push back from the table. Robbie attempts to dive under the table, bumping into Roxi in the process and spilling the drink from her hand. Dmitri stands and attempts to flip the table, unaware that it's solid mahogany. I shout as I see Dmitri grab Roxi and take her down. SWAT team has swarmed the room and a flare goes off with a bang, the brilliant white light casting everything into sharp relief before smoke fills the room. It's Roxi's scream that pulls everything back from slow-motion. "Roxi," I shout. "Are you okay?" I'm being wrestled to the floor, hands yanked behind my back. "Roxi," I shout again, but it's too loud. Everyone is screaming, shouting profanities, yelling in pain. I can't see from the burning in my eyes, and I swear it's gone black. There's a knee, or the butt of a rifle pressing so hard into the center of my back, I think my spine might snap. I hear people being dragged out one by one, and I keep calling for Roxi until I'm hoarse.

When I'm finally jerked to my feet, I gasp at the

amount of smoke in the air. I'm pulled down the hall, and too late, I think of my laptop. At least it's encrypted, but somehow I don't think that's going to be a challenge for this group. I'm blinded by bright lights as I'm hauled into the bar, there have got to be thirty or more Feds swarming the room, pulling down ceiling panels, pulling open drawers, stuffing anything they can find into evidence bags. "Hey, be careful with that," I shout at one person behind the bar who's manhandling vintage stemware. That earns me another hard jerk as I'm propelled toward the door. Oscar is nowhere in sight, and neither are any of the men from the game. "Roxi?" I yell again. "Roxi, where are you? Are you okay? Are you hurt? She's innocent," I shout at someone walking by wearing latex gloves. Fuck, I never should have let her work here. I should have listened to her, or Stockton about the game. I should have listened to my instincts. I should have called the game. I should have booted Vince. The litany in my head goes on, and on, and on. Everything in my whole life I should have done differently, that I didn't, and now it's jeopardized the woman I love.

Chapter Twenty

_T_hey must have separated all of us. I have no idea where anyone is, and I'm alone in the vehicle as it makes its way to wherever the holding center is. There's no point in me talking, the driver is a wall. And my repeated requests for information about Roxi have fallen on deaf ears.

A short time later, I'm pulled from the car and brought into bright lights and sky-blue halls, before my cuffs are released and I'm 'invited' to take a seat in a room with three chairs, a folding table, and a two-way mirror. I have no idea how long I wait. It seems like forever. I fold my arms on the table and rest my head on them. I've read enough thrillers to know how this shit works. I shut my eyes and attempt to take a nap while they're wearing me down. But my mind is like a spinning wheel in a gerbil cage. It won't stop, and all I can think about is Roxi. Is she being held too? Is she okay? Her scream haunts me, and I pray to whatever gods will listen that she's unhurt.

After what feels like ages, a guy comes in. I've seen his type before — thinks he's hot shit, but he's forty-pounds overweight from the stress, losing his hair, and looking to impress his colleagues with his badassery by behaving like a complete and total douchebag.

"You're Danny Pendergast, yes?"

He's spilled coffee on his tie. I contemplate pointing that out to him. "Yes."

"Where were you this evening?"

"This ain't my first rodeo." I know exactly what he's trying to do, and it won't work. He's trying to exact a confession from me, and I've never been so grateful for my experiences as a juvenile delinquent. East side cops are notorious for bending the rules to get a conviction, and I'm a scrappy motherfucker who refuses to play their game. "Sir," I add after a lengthy pause.

I can tell he doesn't like my answer, or my smart remark. But I am not giving him the satisfaction.

"I want to know where my girlfriend is."

"Your girlfriend?"

"Yes. Roxi Rickoli. Redhead. Big boobs."

Surprise registers on his face, but also recognition. He's seen her.

"Where is she?" I press. "I'm not saying anything until I see her. And I swear if any of you hurt her, I'll—"

"You'll what, Mr. Pendergast? May I remind you, you're in federal custody. I don't think you're going to be doing shit. Now why don't you tell me about this little poker game you had going on."

I stare at my hands. A full minute ticks by. "We can do this the easy way, or we can do this the hard way, Mr. Pendergast."

"I'm not going to let you intimidate me. I want to see Roxi."

He curses under his breath and walks out, only to walk

back in five minutes later. "Tell me about the Whiskey Den, Mr. Pendergast."

"Tell me about Roxi." I know my rights. I don't have to say shit.

Mr. Douchebag braces his arm on the table. "You're going to tell me what I need to know and then I'll give you an update on your girlfriend."

The way he says it makes my blood turn to ice. Like something is gravely wrong, but they're using her to bludgeon me into confessing. "What exactly do you want to know?"

"How long have you been using the Whiskey Den to launder money?"

"I don't fucking launder money."

"Your great-grandfather did. Why wouldn't you?"

"Because *I don't launder money.*" I grit. "Now tell me what I'm being charged with or tell me about my girlfriend." I glare at him. "Or get the fuck out of here."

His eyes widen slightly, and again, he tries to intimidate me by leaning over the table. "Let's get one thing straight, Danny-o. You're the one in federal custody. You don't get to call the shots. You cooperate, you'll get to see your girlfriend. Now why don't you tell me what you were doing at the Whiskey Den this evening with Vince Ferrari, Alex Descharmes, Dmitri Sokolov, Stockton Forde, Robert Templeton, Robbie Moran, and… what'd you say your chickie's name was? Roxi?"

"She's innocent," I shout. "She's just my employee. She just makes drinks."

Douchebag Don pounces. "If you're calling her innocent, you're implying you're guilty. Are you, Mr. Pendergast? Guilty?"

The door bursts open. "My client is under no obligation to answer that question or any other. Did you inform him that he had the right to the presence of a lawyer?" I recognize the guy, and the slight hint of a southern accent. He's Steele Conglomerate's house counsel. But his name slips me. He extends his hand. "Jackson Hart. I think we've spoken before in the owner's box."

That's where I've met him. Opening day this past year of the Kansas City Kings. "Thank you for coming. Did Stockton send you?"

"Harrison, too." He turns to the interrogator. "May I have five minutes with my client, please?"

D-bag scowls but gives us the room. Jackson pulls out the chair next to mine and sits. "Ya'll are in a mess of hot water. But it's nothing we can't fix. Now, is there anything you want to tell me?"

I'm sure as hell not telling him or anyone else that I was hosting poker. "I want to know why I'm being held. Why the fuck were we raided?"

"I'm still trying to work that out. What are your dealings with the men at tonight's game?"

"Strictly professional. They're all members except for Alex and Robbie, but I vetted their finances and background personally. They all have money."

"Given the questions I've fielded so far for Stockton and Robbie, it sounds like they have inside information on you and the others who were at the table tonight."

"I don't understand."

"It looks like they're after you, or more than one of you for money laundering. I won't know until they make formal charges. They're trying to intimidate any one of you into disclosing a smoking bullet."

Dread pools in my belly as I think back to this afternoon. But Roxi was just putting away her weapon. And my laptop is encrypted. I need to see Roxi. I need to make sure she's okay. "I'll answer any questions you let me answer, so

TESSA LAYNE

long as they let me see with my own eyes that Roxi is okay. In the chaos, she screamed with pain. I need to know she's okay."

Jackson's eyes turn sympathetic. "Are you sure? You don't have to say anything unless you're formally charged, and then only in court."

"I'll make a deal, but only after I've had the chance to see Roxi with my own eyes."

"Let me see what I can do."

A few minutes later he returns. "Well?"

"They're working on it. In the meantime, let's go over what they can and can't ask, and what's your best defense.

Chapter Twenty-One

I've lost all sense of time. But I don't care about anything but seeing Roxi. And I'm done talking with these assholes until I see her with my own eyes. Jackson clears his throat, but I don't need any more coaching. I raise a hand. "We can talk after I see Roxi."

"They've gone to fetch her, but I wouldn't be doing my job if I didn't tell you to not say anything to her. She's a material witness at the very least, they could be holding something over her head and using her to get to you."

I strike the table. "She is *not* a mole."

"You don't know that."

"Like hell I don't," I growl, done with this shit. He's right though, I've seen Feds turn innocent people into weapons because they're scared shitless. This is so far above Roxi's pay grade it's not funny. "Can you check on her? Give her advice?"

Jackson shakes his head. "I don't know Roxi and representing her might come into conflict with whatever I need to do for you and Stockton."

"But someone needs to help her. She's got no one on her side. She's probably scared shitless."

Jackson sighs heavily. "If I see her in the hall, I'll remind her she doesn't have to say anything without the presence of a lawyer. I can recommend someone in my firm."

His assurances ease the knot in my chest, but only a little. Jackson steps out, and the door clicks shut behind him with an ominous snick. The minutes tick by, and in that time, I replay every choice I've made that's led me to this point. I'll give it all up, every penny, if it means that Roxi is okay. I sag with relief when the door opens and she slips in, left arm in a sling.

I leap from the chair and round the table. "Tell me you're okay," I say, taking her by the shoulders and pulling her close to press a kiss to her temple. "Did you see Stockton's lawyer? I sent him to come find you. You don't owe these assholes anything. Don't say a word to them without a lawyer present. You haven't done anything wrong, so don't let them convince you otherwise." She nods, face buried in my chest, but something's off. Very off. "Roxi? What is it, sweetheart?"

She looks at me, and the anguish I see on her face slices through me like a knife. My stomach drops to my toes. "We need to talk," she says in a shaky voice.

"Of course." Dread turns my veins to ice. Something is very, very wrong. "What is it, did they already talk to you?" I've never seen her look like this, like a caged animal. Afraid. *Guilty.* "What did you tell them Roxi? What did they force you to say? I swear, if they——"

"*Sit.* Danny. Just. Sit. Down," she grits, a look of utter defeat passing across her face.

I pull out a chair for her, then round the table to where the other two chairs are at angles. I reach across the table and take her right hand. "What happened?" I motion to the sling.

She gives me a crooked smile. "Just a flesh wound. Vince had a knife, and in the chaos, I got nicked."

"I'll kill him," I growl.

Her voice turns razor sharp. "*Don't...* say things like that."

"I mean it. If he ever lays a finger on you—"

"No. *I* mean it. Don't say shit like that. You'll—" She hangs her head, and her words come out just above a whisper. "You'll just make it worse."

My stomach clenches. "What's going on Roxi?"

She looks tortured, and a part of me goes frantic, like there's nothing I can do to help her, to protect her. "Danny, whatever they're asking you, you need to cooperate. Fully."

"What do you mean?"

"They know about the games. Your best option is to cooperate when they ask."

"Did they get to you already? What did you tell them Roxi?"

She shakes her head. "I didn't tell them anything they didn't already know," she says, voice tight. "Just... *please.* Promise me you'll cooperate."

"It will cost me everything if I don't fight this. My reputation will be ruined. I have clients I need to consider."

She shoots a deathly glare at me. "And what about yourself? Are you saying you'd rather go to prison than cooperate? What about your mother? And-and Polly?" Her voice grows thick with emotion. "And the other people who count on you to be steady. And true. What about them?"

I hear the implied *me* in her accusation. *What about me?* But why doesn't she ask it? "Don't you mean what about us?" I snap. "You knew what you were getting into when we crossed the line."

Her mouth twists into a bitter smile. "Yes. I guess I did." She fists her uninjured hand on the table. "And here's the awful thing. I love you Danny. I don't want you to go to prison. I want you to cooperate with the Feds and stay the hell out of this mess. I don't care if you lose everything, because I want to come home to you at night, not talk to you through a piece of fucking glass." Her voice is brittle. Desperate even.

"What are they holding over you, Rox? Let me help you. Don't say anything more to those bastards without a lawyer. You haven't done anyth—"

My tirade is interrupted by a knock at the door, and a young man I haven't seen before, although he smells like a Fed, pokes his head in. "Agent Reynolds?"

Agent Reynolds? Time slows to a crawl. Color drains from Roxi's face. In slow motion, I see her turn and give a shake of her head. I hear the exchange, but it all sounds like it's underwater. Baby face speaks first. "Chief Watson needs to see you."

She shakes her head, mouth thinning. "He can wait."

With a ripping sound like a needle scraping across a record, reality comes crashing in. All the unanswered questions, the tiny red flags I ignored all merge together to create an awful picture. Heat rushes through my body, but my hands turn cold. My chest is so tight I can't breathe. My stomach churns and turns upside down even though I haven't eaten for hours. The worst moment is the searing pain of betrayal that threatens to tear out my insides, and my heart along with it.

As soon as the door clicks shut, I rise. "Who the *fuck* are you?"

"I can explain—"

I don't give her the chance. "I already have a damned good picture. This explains everything — why I couldn't find you online, your-your fucking firearm, the martial arts... Jesus," I shout. "You fucking played me from the get-go. Didn't you?"

"Can you sit? Let me explain."

There's a desperation in her voice I should listen to, but I'm too fucking angry. And I'm not about to sit and give her the power in the room. No fucking way. "*Didn't you?*" I shout. "Just say it. You marked me." I pound the table.

"Yes," she shouts back, rising. "I did. But not from the get-go. That was just us. I swear. I-I didn't know who you were that first night. Or-or that you were central to our investigation."

I concentrate on the white-hot anger burning in my chest, use it to calm myself and narrow my focus. "So everything that happened in Napa, that was just bullshit?"

"*No,*" she cries out vehemently with a shake of her head. "I meant every word I said. I love you Danny. Don't you understand? I wasn't supposed to fall in love. Can't you see why this is so hard."

"I can't see why someone who says they love me *would lie to me.*"

"*Because I had a job to do.*"

What's awful? Is that some sick part of me gets that. But I refuse to give her quarter. Not after the way she's used me and made a mockery of our relationship. "So tell me, *Agent Reynolds*, is Roxi even your name?" Her face falls, and that tells me all I need to know. I raise a hand. "*Don't...* tell me. I don't want to know. Just tell me this. Why me?"

"I work in cyber-crimes,"she says, voice full of resignation. "I can tell you, we're after bigger fish than you."

"Who?"

"I'm not at liberty to say."

"Fuck that." I bang the table again.

"Danny, please. If you're willing to cooperate, you'll receive full immunity."

"So if I become a *rat* to save my own skin, is what you're saying."

"Isn't that better than prison?"

"I'm not sure I've committed any felonies. I'll have to discuss it with my lawyer."

She braces her good arm on the table. "Taking a cut from a poker game isn't a felony, but money laundering and bank fraud are."

She's trying to scare me. She's just doing her job to go after whatever bigger fish they want. But fuck. That. She's used me enough. "Get. Out." I say, voice cold.

"Danny, please. I can help you," she pleads.

If she hadn't already ripped out my heart, it might have worked. But I'm dead. "Out," I roar, kicking one of the chairs.

She takes a step back with a nod and a sniff. She rolls her lips together and nods again. "I'll send in your lawyer." She opens the door and pauses, swiveling back to me. "I never meant to hurt you," she says thickly. "You have to believe that."

I turn my back. I'd rather stare at blue painted cement. I want to remember Roxi the way she looked under me this morning when we were making love —face flushed, eyes glazed, smile wide as we moved together. As I made stupid promises about babies and forever. Fuck. Me. I press my forehead to the wall. A shudder wracks me, but I refuse to give in. I haven't cried since I was sixteen. I'm not about to start now. But I'm quite sure the hole she's left in my heart will never heal.

Chapter Twenty-Two

In the end, and at Jackson's recommendation, I take the deal. But not because of Roxi. No, I have bigger fish to fry, too. It turns out the Feds were after Ferrari and Sokolov for human trafficking, and Stockton's instincts were right on. Too bad they came a little too late. But I'm pissed as hell at the way those assholes used me. In all fairness, I used them too, but not to abuse women, and I want those fuckers to rot for that. I'm not sure I'll ever forgive myself for not paying closer attention to them. My stomach still churns with disgust at the thought he might have been marking Roxi for trafficking, or worse, that they were trafficking women right under my nose.

A knock sounds at my door at the same time my phone rings. I glance at the clock. Six-fucking-thirty. Who the fuck is harassing me at this hour? And on a goddamned Saturday? The phone rings again. Harrison. "What?" I snarl into the phone. "This better be good."

"Open your fucking door, asswipe," he snaps back.

I throw on a pair of sweats and pad through the loft to

the door. "It's still fucking dark out," I say as I throw open the door.

Harrison's in gym clothes and holding a tray of coffee. Behind him Stockton waves. "Happy New Year, man."

"Fuck you." I step aside to let them in. "Have either of you been to bed?"

Stockton shoots me an evil grin as he heads to the kitchen table. "We've been planning."

"Can you share the details at noon?" But I know better. Once these guys get an idea, they're like a pair of goddamned terriers fighting over a rope.

"New year, new life," answers Harrison. "Training starts in an hour."

"At seven-thirty on New Year's Day?" I ask, incredulous. "Training for *what?*"

"A spot opened up on the boat. Trevor got a promotion that's taking him to Boston," Stockton supplies. "We've got to work overtime to bring you up to speed."

"I haven't said yes."

Harrison raises his coffee. "That's okay. We said yes for you." I start to object, but he cuts me off. "You've been moping since all this shit went down, when really you ought to be celebrating that your ass isn't in jail and that the forensic accountants assigned to your case were able to salvage half your fortune."

"Too bad they couldn't salvage my reputation," I gripe. "Even if I were to reinvest what I have left, I've lost everyone's trust."

"Not ours," states Stockton, a serious expression on his face. "We have a proposal for you, but it's contingent on you saying yes to joining our boat."

"That sounds an awful lot like blackmail."

Harrison gives me a look that only a CEO of a multinational conglomerate can pull off. "I prefer to frame it as an *opportunity*. An above board, *legitimate* opportunity. But if you want to consider it blackmail, we can call it that, too."

It's too early for this shit. My brain feels dull, my synapses aren't firing together. I take another gulp of coffee and wipe my mouth with the back of my hand. "Okay, fine. Pitch it."

Stockton's eyes light as he leans forward, looking to Harrison for the go-ahead. "Provided you say yes to rowing with us again, we'd like you to buy into the Kansas City Kings ownership group."

I take a minute to let that sink in. "But I'm not a baseball fan." Roxi is, I remember with a twinge in my sternum. And I promised her a game.

"You don't have to be," Harrison reassures me. "Although I'm pretty proud of our guys. This is a purely financial decision."

"So at the risk of sounding like an asshole, what's in it for me?"

"I'm glad you asked." Stockton slides a folder across the table.

"What's this?" I take the folder. Inside are schematics for a distillery on the center right-field landing called King Tom's. An anchor business and a tribute to my great-grandfather. "So you want me to start distilling again." I'm at a loss for words. I haven't been able to see the forest through the trees since Roxi's betrayal, and yeah, I get it could have been much, much worse, but losing her, losing what I thought we had, took the wind out of my sails.

Harrison clears his throat. "You need to get back in the boat. You need to remember you've got a team of friends pulling with you."

How can I say no? The choice is clear, and they've made it damn easy to say yes. "What's your timeline?"

"We have the equipment in place. There's some basic

design and construction work that needs to be done, but we think it can be ready by opening day."

"But whiskey won't be ready by then."

Harrison and Stockton exchange a glance. "As part-owners of the Whiskey Den, we were able to claim the barrels as our own."

I'm not entirely sure that's above board, but if anyone can find a loophole it's Jackson. And given the Feds have crawled over all of my assets and then some, if they parted with the barrels, then lucky me. "Okay. I'll do it."

Stockton raises his cup. "Welcome to the club. We have a press release ready to go at ten this morning."

"You were that sure I'd say yes?"

Harrison looks way too satisfied with himself. "Yep. And now we have to get to the gym, because Sparky's there, waiting to kick your ass into high gear."

It'll hurt, training up to row again. It'll be fucking agony. It won't mend the hole in my heart, but it's a step to rebuilding my life.

Mariah — aka Sparky — is waiting for us. "Welcome to the team, Danny," she says with an evil grin.

"Your smile is making me nervous."

She waggles her eyebrows. "It should. I love nothing more than fresh meat. And you're about to discover I've been letting you off easy."

"Bring it."

Twenty-minutes later, I regret ever challenging Sparky to bring it, as I sit with my head over a bucket, heaving the coffee Harrison gave me.

Mariah laughs maniacally, and hands me a towel along with a cup of water. "Don't gulp it."

"Jeezus. Now I remember everything I hated about rowing."

"It'll get better," Harrison says, clapping me on the back. "Think of this as a rite of passage."

"Yeah, yeah. New Year, new me. Fuck that shit. I wanna go back to bed."

"So you can lie around all day and be depressed? Fuck *that* shit."

He's right. I need to move on, and my friends have supplied the perfect opportunity. I towel my face and glance up to see a picture of Vincent on the T.V. "Hey guys, check it out. Turn it up?"

Sparky grabs the remote and turns up the volume. The announcer's voice comes through the loudspeakers. "*In a stunning turn of events, yesterday, a federal grand jury indicted Vincent Ferrari on first-degree murder charges of a seventeen-year-old cold case involving the murder of Loyola University Chicago college student Colleen Reynolds. Ferrari is currently in custody for pending charges of money laundering and human trafficking.*"

A picture of a young blonde with curly hair flashes on the screen. I remember looking at that picture and ruling it out after Roxi shared that her sister had been murdered. *Because I'd been looking for a Rickoli.* It never occurred to me that Roxi wasn't who she claimed to be. "Turn it off," I snap, while I take off toward the other side of the gym. Fuck. *Fuck. Fuck. Fuck.* Puzzle pieces drop into my head like dominoes, creating a picture I don't want to acknowledge, because then it would absolve Roxi of so much, and I'm not ready for that.

"What the fuck, man?" Harrison asks when I return to them. "You look like you've seen a ghost."

"That girl," I point to the T.V. "Is, *was* Roxi's sister. I'd bet the last of my money on it."

"Are you sure?" asks Stockton, expression skeptical. "That's a mighty big coincidence."

"She's our age. And she mentioned her older sister had been murdered when she was fifteen."

"Okay, so the math works out, but that doesn't mean it's Roxi's sister."

"Except, when I was in holding, a Fed came in and called her Agent Reynolds."

Harrison lets out a low whistle. A glance at Stockton tells me he's already mathing the odds. But he shakes his head. "I don't know. Are you sure you're not grasping at straws?"

"Who's got a phone?"

Both the guys shake their heads, pointing to the locker room, but Sparky offers hers up. I do a quick search for *Colleen Reynolds Obituary Loyola*. Half a dozen hits come up. The top hit is from a suburb of Chicago. I wrack my brain trying to remember if Roxi mentioned where her dad lives. I pull up the obit, scanning for any crumb that supports my theory. "She was a journalism student. Maybe she was doing some kind of investigative piece." I keep reading. "Colleen is survived by her father Sean, her stepmother Marsha, and half-sister Jane." The fledgling butterfly of hope tentatively beating its wings against my chest evaporates to dust. Nothing in the obit points to this being Roxi. She never mentioned her dad by name. Or her mother. Or that her sister had a different mother.

Stockton and Harrison exchange a glance. "I'm sorry, man." Stockton says, breaking the silence.

I wave him off. "Shut it." My chest throbs like I've been stabbed. And even though it's been weeks, I'm living Roxi's betrayal all over again. It's not like lemon juice in a paper cut — fuck, that would be a goddamn walk in the park. It's not even like walking barefoot across glass. Maybe I'd equate this with having my fingernails pulled out. Not the worst thing I've endured, but pretty damned close. "Are we done here?" I finally ask when I can't take their pitying stares anymore.

"Training is at six-thirty every morning except Thursdays and Sundays. Those are your recovery days, but I expect you to run a 5k. Minimum. Core workout and light weights are okay too. Make sure your diet is high in protein, healthy fats, and complex carbs. You're now training to be a high-performance athlete. Minimal booze, no smoking or banned substances, and adequate sleep." She eyes Harrison and Stockton as she says this last bit. "You burn the candle at both ends, it's going to impact your performance."

"Understood." I give her a salute. "If you gents are planning on more torture, I'll Uber back. I'm throwing in the towel today."

"We're headed out to Mason and Luci's for posole. You want to join us and meet the other owners?"

I'm pretty sure I've seen most of them at my club at one time or another. "I have a date with a hot shower and Tinder."

Stockton's eyes widen. "Are you sure?"

"It's either Tinder or the Humane Society. New Year, new me, right?" I say with a heavy dose of sarcasm, but it's enough to get them off my back.

I fixate on the idea of a dog. I scan the Humane Society website as the Uber whisks me the ten-minute drive from the Briarcliff to the Crossroads. As soon as I push open the door to my penthouse, I stop, hair on the back of my neck rising. Something's off. I scan the hallway. Nothing seems out of place, but my spidey sense is going crazy. "Fuck, I *do* need a dog," I mutter to myself as I make my way to the kitchen. It's not even nine a.m. I could turn on the Rose Parade, I could make a breakfast cocktail, or I could go back to bed. Bed sounds pretty damned inviting.

I decide on a recovery shake and sleep. I make my way to the kitchen but stop short when I spy a guest sitting at my table, rearranging the coffee cups leftover from my conversation with the boys a few hours earlier. "What the fuck are you doing here?"

Chapter Twenty-Three

*A*ll the hurt comes rushing back into my chest when I see Roxi sitting at my table. In spite of that, I take her in like a man starved for nourishment. She looks… like water in the desert. If I'm critical, I can see that her cheeks are hollowed — like she hasn't been eating enough. Her mouth is pinched, and her eyes have lost the sparkle that made my stomach do flip-flops. Her hair's pulled back into a low ponytail, and she's wearing a leather motorcycle jacket over jeans and a white tee-shirt. But damn if she isn't as lovely as always, in spite of the stress she wears.

She flashes me a tentative smile and opens her arms. "I'm not armed."

"What are you doing here, Roxi?" I'm wary. How could I not be? The last time we saw each other, I was in a holding cell, life crumbling around my ears.

"I… ah… wanted to return your key." She pushes it to the center of the table.

"You could have mailed it."

"I know," she says in a small voice. "I was hoping—"

She shakes her head and sighs. "I also wanted to give you this." She pushes a Manila envelope forward. "I wanted you to know the whole truth."

"How thoughtful of you." She winces at the sarcasm in my voice.

"I'm not sure if you saw the news yet. But—"

"I did."

She pats the envelope. "There are several pictures of me and Colleen— her high school graduation. The two of us the Christmas before she died."

"Stop." I hold up a hand. "I read the obit, Roxi. We both know it's not you."

She shoots me a look full of anger and anguish. "I've also enclosed both my birth certificate and a copy of my passport," she says, voice trembling. "I was born Roxanna Jane Reynolds. Thanks to Sting, I was teased mercilessly about my name. When I was ten, I asked everyone to start calling me Jane." She digs into her pocket. "Here's my driver's license." She tosses it on top of the envelope.

"Feds can make you any I.D. you want."

"They can. But I have no reason to lie to you. Not anymore," she adds in a whisper, pink flushing her cheeks. "Lastly, someone I know who's working on Ferrari's case did me a favor before I left. My sister was a journalism major, and unbeknownst to us, was working on a human trafficking exposé that involved college campuses. Ferrari thought she was getting too close. But when they raided his lair, they found a safe with... trophies." She grimaces. "There was a thumb drive in his safe with her article that was set to print the week she died."

It's a fantastic story. But how can I believe it when she's betrayed my trust like she has?

"I wasn't about to cost my co-worker his job, but he at least let me view the article."

"Why are you telling me this?"

"Because I want you to know the full truth," she snaps. "There will be another indictment handed down tomorrow. The suicide of Colleen's journalism advisor three months after she died has now been ruled a homicide."

I fight to hold onto my anger, my hurt. "You make a compelling case. But why now? Why not when you first found out?"

"Because as of last week, I no longer work for the Bureau."

Whoa. I let that bombshell sink in. But I don't know what to say, because it's not like I even fucking knew.

She continues. "And… in light of that, I've decided it's time to move back home. To Downer's Grove, outside of Chicago. I think my parents could use some extra support right now."

Her news lands like a punch to the gut. I realize that even though we've been apart, that I don't move through the city without thinking of her, of imagining where she is or what she might be doing. The thought of her gone for good… is unsettling. "What will you do there?"

She picks at her thumbnail. "There's not much work for forensic accountants outside of the F.B.I." She lets out a humorless laugh. "Good thing I know how to tend bar."

"But why not stay here, and visit more frequently?" It's a selfish request, I know. My closest friends all have family in the area, and I'd never consent to living across the country with mom still in nursing care. But I can't help but hope she might want to stay for something else.

She looks straight at me, agony written in every line on her face. "There's nothing left for me here."

My stomach hollows. There's nothing left for her because I told her to go away. "What if there were? Something here? Would you stay?"

She shuts her eyes, as if she's trying valiantly to keep her shit together. The look in her eyes when she opens them nearly breaks me with its bleakness. "I don't expect you to forgive me for keeping secrets."

"You mean lying."

"Fine. Lying. I don't expect you to forgive me. I won't be so bold as to ask for it. But I do hope you can understand how desperately I want justice for Colleen. I studied math, then forensic accounting with the sole goal of getting into the F.B.I. so I could find her killer. This has been the single focus of my life since the day we got the awful call. It wasn't until I was sent into the Whiskey Den that I realized we'd met before. And I should have recused myself right then and there. Disclosed that we'd already... er... met. But I wanted in on bringing down Ferrari." She blushes, color racing from her neck to her hairline.

"But why couldn't you have told them you knew me?"

"I'm really good at what I do — finding needles in cyber haystacks." Her face turns beet red. "I knew if I was on the inside, I could hack into the accounting system you used, and with the information I discovered, I knew I could trace Ferrari's transactions — not just to the Whiskey Den, but to ... other places."

"You hacked my computer? Jesus, Roxi." I run a hand through my hair."

"Only your books. I swear I didn't look at anything else."

I snort. "Honor among thieves?"

"I was jut doing my job. And I knew I could do it better than anyone else. And if my bosses knew that we'd... um..." she waves between us.

"Fucked like rabid bunnies in the restroom?" My mouth turns up at the absurdity of it all.

"Something like that," she mumbles, face still bright

with embarrassment. "They'd have kept me off this assign-ment. There was a tenuous link that Ferrari was related to Colleen's murder and I wasn't going to pass up that chance." She sucks in a ragged breath, and instinctively I brace myself for more bombshells. "And I wanted to see you again," she whispers, dropping her gaze. "I… wanted more."

"I suppose I should feel flattered," I say wryly.

"I didn't count on falling in love with you." She draws a circle with her finger on the envelope, still keeping her gaze averted. "I regret not being able to tell you. More than anything. And you have to know that I wanted to. I regret hurting you. But I don't regret bringing in Ferrari. And—" she glances up. "I don't regret for a second anything that happened between us." She grimaces. "Everything I said about how I felt— how I *feel*, is the truth. I love you."

"And that's why you're leaving?" I snap, jaw clenching tight.

"I'm leaving because I couldn't continue the lies at my job anymore than I could live with the lies I had to tell you. You are without a doubt, the best thing that has ever happened in my life. And I stupidly, *naively* thought I could have both you and justice for my sister." Her voice grows thick with tears. "You are a good man, Danny. And some-day, I know you'll find someone worthy of your love, and who sees what a good man you are." She sucks in a ragged breath. "But I can't be here when that happens, because it will remind me of everything I lost."

She rises and taps the envelope. "Read it, don't read it. Tear it up, burn it. It's yours to do with as you wish." She takes a deep breath and promptly lets it out. "Thank you for hearing me out." Her smile is forced. "I'll let myself out." She slips by me, and I make no move to stop her, mind reeling with everything she laid out. The click of the door sliding shut echoes with a finality that resonates in my bones. I'm not sure how long I stand there, leaning against the wall and staring at the Manila envelope, half waiting for it to self-destruct.

Curiosity gets the better of me, and I snatch it off the table, fumbling with the brad and shaking out the contents. All it takes is one look at the first picture — an awkward pubescent Roxi grinning at the camera, already showing hints of the woman to come, squeezing a smiling Colleen — for it to hit home in the deepest part of me that she was telling the truth about everything.

I drop to my knees with a cry, pain knifing through me, searing like a lightning bolt. The rawness of it calls up a long-buried memory. Of when I learned my mother would never recover from the beating my father delivered. That I would never hear her laughter, or feel her hand on my cheek, or see the pride in her eyes when she looked at me. Gone forever, doomed to live in a shell of a body. And me, only sixteen with no means to care for her. How much worse to learn the sister you loved, the daughter of your heart, would never come home?

I *hate* that I was collateral damage. But I understand. And I would like to personally be in the cell with Vince so that I can rip his balls off one at a time, not that it would in any way, shape, or form pay for the harm he's inflicted on so many young women. In time, my anger will fade. My hurt will heal.

Because I love Roxi.

And the thought of her not in my life hurts far worse than the pain she's caused. And fuck — I let her go. I let her walk the fuck out of my house thinking she was walking out of my life for good. The realization pulls me to my feet. What if she planned to leave today? Drive home in time for dinner? If she left now, she'd be in Chicagoland by dinner. I tear out of the penthouse and take the stairs two at a time — there's no time to wait for the elevator. My legs are burning when I push out the exit and stumble onto the sidewalk. There's only one place she could be if she's still in town. I jog to the car, and too late, realize the fob is still in the entryway upstairs. "Happy Fucking New Year," I mutter as I break into a sprint. I better earn extra brownie points from Sparky for this tomorrow.

The house on the West Side is a little over a mile away, and I push myself, picking up the pace. I make it to her front steps in less than ten minutes, and I've never been so relieved to see her car in the drive. My relief dissipates when I spy the for sale sign in the pocket yard. Fuck. She really means to leave town. I march over to the sign and yank it from the ground. This is my John Cusack moment. If I had a boom box, I'd raise it high. And since the grocer is still closed at this hour, eliminating the possibility of flowers, the sign's the best I can do. I leap up the steps, offering a silent prayer that she's here. I bang on the screen door. "Roxi. You there?"

Ten seconds tick by.

Then twenty.

I bang again. "Roxi?"

The door cracks open.

"Roxi?"

Then it swings wide, and Roxi's there, as beautiful and magnificent as ever, albeit with red-rimmed eyes. Her eyes go wide as her face registers surprise, then confusion.

I hold up the sign before she has the chance to push me away. "Don't go?"

She cocks her head, brows knitting together.

"This *is* your house, isn't it? You weren't housesitting, were you?"

She looks pained as she nods. "I'm sorry about that, too."

"That's not why I'm here. I…" The words tangle up in the back of my throat. The odds of me coming off like a total dumbass are fairly high. I take a deep breath. "I love you Roxanna Jane Reynolds. I want to be in your life. I want you to be in mine. I… please don't go. Stay?"

Chapter Twenty-Four

My heart pounds in my throat as she stares at me for what feels like eternity. In spite of my best efforts, flutterings of hope stir in my chest. The flutters flame to life when she pushes open the screen with a cry, cups my face and lays a kiss on me.

It's all her, teasing my mouth open and sliding her tongue against mine. Our mouths mold together like magnets finding home, and I pour all of my inarticulate feelings into the kiss, telling her everything my words fail to describe. She drops her forehead to mine, when we pull apart.

"So… is that a yes?"

"Umm-hmm."

I step back only far enough to lean the sign against the railing, and back her up to the door so I can kiss her properly. A car honks as it passes.

"Come inside." She laces her fingers through mine and pulls me through the door, turning to lock it as soon as I've crossed the threshold.

"Nice digs," I say, looking around. The decor is urban

modern, but cozier than my place. Homier. A streak of orange flashes by me. I catch a glimpse of a bushy tail before it dives under the couch. "You have a cat?" I say pointing to where I saw the tail. "Or was it a raccoon?"

"That's Sweetie Pie." She smirks, waiting for me to respond.

I take the bait. "You named your cat Sweetie Pie?"

She nods. "I was going to call it that all the time, anyway. So why not?"

I flick my eyebrows. "Indeed."

Silence stretches between the two of us. And we both end up speaking at once.

"Coffee?" she says.

"Where's your bedroom?" I ask.

She cocks her head, brows furrowed. "What did you say?"

I close the space between us, pulling the hand I still hold to my mouth and kissing each knuckle. "I said," letting my kisses punctuate the words. "Where is your bedroom? We never got to have make-up sex. I figured now might be as good a time as any to start."

Her mouth twitches. "Make-up sex."

I nod. "We could call it 'let's get reacquainted sex,' too. If you like that better," I add.

"I like sex," she says, grinning broadly now, hands fluttering at the hem of her shirt.

"Are you fucking with me?" I peel off my jacket.

"Maybe just a little." I blink, and her shirt has joined my jacket on the floor. Her bra is a pale-yellow lace that perfectly complements her creamy, freckled skin.

"Show me your panties," I say, voice turning to gravel as a shock of awareness rolls through me. I've missed this sensation, the anticipation of untold delight, of sweaty bodies and tangled limbs, of a feast both visual and oral.

"Demanding, aren't you?"

"It's been awhile."

"Indeed," she shoots back at me with the same tone of voice I used moments before.

My control begins to fray. "Panties off, sweetheart, or I will toss you over my shoulder and take you upstairs where I will personally remove them, and they might not survive."

Her grin widens and then she bites her lip, eyes sparkling with expectation. "Promise?"

Chapter Twenty-Five

*pening Day*

The excitement is tangible as Roxi and I pull into the owner's lot at Royal Field in the East Bottoms. The team is coming off three consecutive wins at Spring Training, and two days of feel-good publicity from the annual Pros and Veterans charity game over in Prairie. But I'm excited for half-a-dozen other reasons. Namely the enormous diamond ring that's burning a hole in my pocket. Oh yeah, and the grand opening of King Tom's Distillery.

"Stay here." I jog around the front, open her door, and offer my hand. Roxi's eyes light up when she sees the vintage brick exterior modeled after Camden Yards. "Dad's gonna flip when he sees this," she says with her signature enthusiastic grin.

"Your mom texted and said they'd be here in an hour." It was Harrison who gave me the idea of proposing on

Opening Day. Roxi wasn't suspicious at all when I rang up her parents about coming down for the game. The conversation wasn't as awkward as I'd anticipated, given I've only met her parents once. But for all the rules we've broken, I wanted to do this by the book.

"Why are we here so early again?"

I wrap my arm around her waist and pull her close as we approach the owner's entrance and flash our credentials. "Harrison wanted all the owners here early to schmooze. And once we've walked the field and congratulated the team, Harrison suggested a private celebration at the Distillery before the official ribbon-cutting."

Roxi leans her head on my shoulder. "So long as I'm with you, I'm game for anything."

And then it hits me, how I'm going to propose. "So would you make the first round of cocktails?"

She lets out a giggle. "Were you planning that all along?"

"Nope. You should know by now I'm more of a spontaneous guy."

She looks around. "In that case, is there somewhere we can sneak off for a grand-slam?" she says with a smirk and an eye waggle.

"I think it's called the seventh-inning stretch."

"We have to wait that long?" Her lower lip juts out in a pout.

"Patience, grasshopper," I say giving her ass a pinch. "Thank you for wearing a skirt, by the way. I'll be sure to slip my hand between your thighs at the first home run."

"Promise?"

The mood in the owner's box is lively. Mason Carter's wife, Luci has laid out a taco bar, and Lisa, wearing Polly in a wrap-around sling, has set up both a Mimosa bar *and* a

Bloody Mary bar. "Watch out for the ghost-pepper infused tequila," she warns with a wink. Harrison, Stockton, and Owen, Steele Conglomerate's CFO and another crew-mate, are out on the balcony smoking cigars. I leave Roxi briefly to join them.

Harrison claps me on the back. "So glad you've joined us."

"This is our year," Stockton adds with a gleam in his eye. "I had Felicity run predictive analytics based on Spring Training. I predict we're on top of the AL Central by the All-Star game."

"Anyone want to wager on that?" Owen asks with a wink.

"Sorry," I say with a tiny bit of chagrin. "My betting days are done. Unless we're betting which one of you assholes is going to be the next to get married."

Their reactions are priceless. Harrison's jaw ticks, Stockton looks like he swallowed an ice-cube whole, and Owen is suddenly very interested in the wood grain along the balcony railing. Harrison clears his throat. "Let's just see how it goes with you. You ready?"

I nod. "I'm all in. As soon as Roxi's parents arrive we can make our way to the distillery."

I slip back inside and wrap an arm around Roxi while she's cuddling Polly. "She looks good in your arms," I murmur.

The look Roxi gives me is full of heat. "She looks cuter in your arms. Do you want to hold her?"

"I'll claim her for tickles and tosses a little later. Have your folks arrived?"

"Yes. Mason is giving them the tour, he suggested we meet up at the distillery?

The time passes slower than watching sloth videos on

National Geographic. At last, we make our way to the distillery on the center-right field landing. The aroma of fermenting mash tickles my nose. Sweet and faintly sour, it's a scent that will forever bring a smile to my face. The pot stills are shiny and bright, and the far wall is lined with barrels. In the center are several high-top tables where people can sit or stand and watch the game through the enormous picture windows, or on any of the T.V.s that hang from the ceiling. The bar is set up on the wall facing the barrels, so that even the bartenders have a view of the game. Outside, is a small balcony filled with umbrella tables so people can sit outside and watch the game in the open air. I wish I could say the concept was my own, but this was all the Harrison and Owen.

I pull Roxi behind the bar. "How about a round of Old Fashioneds? For old-time's sake?"

"Not whiskey, neat?" she teases.

"Second round."

She sets to work. "Help me with the garnishes?"

"Of course." I feel for the outline of the ring in my front pocket, nerves getting the best of me. I set to work peeling lemon and orange rind, and stabbing Amarena cherries with toothpicks. We work well together, like we always have, one instinctively offering what the other needs. We line the drinks up on the bar and invite everyone to grab a glass.

I slip the ring onto the toothpick in the glass closest to Roxi, and make a quick search for her dad, who gives a little nod of approval. I raise my glass. "Six months ago, almost to the day, I woke up and went through a very ordinary day. At about ten-minutes before seven that night, winds of change blew into my life in the form of the most beautiful spirit I've ever met." I glance over to Roxi and give her hand a squeeze. "I couldn't have predicted any of the upheaval that followed. Nor could I predict that not only would I find a partner in life and love, but that in spite of the obstacles thrown at us, our love managed to grow. I hope that's a sign of good things to-"

"*OhmygodwhatisTHAT?*" She interrupts my awkward speech with a squeal, staring wide-eyed at her cocktail. "Are you *proposing* Danny?"

I drop a knee to the rubber mat. "I'm definitely proposing, and yes, dear, that's a diamond ring in your cocktail." I take the glass from her shaking hand and remove the ring and hold it out to her. "Roxi Rickoli will you marry me?"

"Only if you get her name right," hollers her father from the other side of the bar, eliciting a roar of laughter from our friends.

"I don't care what you call me," she says, holding out her finger to receive the ring. "The answer's yes. Yes. Yes. Yes."

I don't hear the cheering and clapping as I stand and pull her into my arms, dipping her for a kiss that quickly turns hot. She has my complete attention, like she has from the very beginning. And like she will in the years to come.

THE BEGINNING OF HAPPILY EVER AFTER

I hope you enjoyed reading Danny and Roxi's story. Are you ready for more sinfully sexy romance? Pre-order PU$$Y MAGNET today. It's the first book in my new Titans of Tech series. The Titans are bossy, they're hot and they'll melt your eReader.

Harrison Steele

Let's get one thing straight. I love pu$$y. Effin'. Love. It.

Call me shallow, call me a perv, call me a cocky bastard, but the reason I know there's a heaven is because God made women.

Because no matter who a woman is, a ball-buster in the courtroom or a flower child at an Avitt Brothers concert, I have the keys to their kingdom, and they all want it.

Until Mariah Sanchez - aka Sparky

She wants me.

I can feel it. I can *smell* it. But for nine months, sixteen days, twelve hours and forty-seven minutes she's had my "you know what" in irons. Worse, my mouth and my fingers, too. Locked up in an invisible prison of my own making. And because I'm a stupid idiot, the only person I can blame for my predicament is me.

But that's about to change…

Order PU$$Y MAGNET now!!

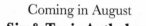

Coming in August

Sin & Tonic Anthology

Including the Pu$$y Magnet prequel…

Bar, pub, speakeasy, tavern, cocktail lounge. What do all these have in common?

They're places for drinking, places for talking, places for meeting, and in this anthology, they're places to fall in love.

Pull up a seat, grab a drink, and enter the worlds of four romance authors for some steamy heroes, strong heroines, and sexy-as-hell sin. Cocktail recipes to seduce your sweetie included!

Wild Thang- USA Today Bestselling Author, Tessa Layne

When billionaire Mason Carter discovers his longtime crush Luci Cruz has packed her bags and is leaving town forever, he's got twenty-four hours to convince her to take one last chance on love. Will a wild night at a notorious speakeasy and a trip down memory lane be enough to win her heart?

All In- USA Today Bestselling Author, Mira Lyn Kelly

There ought to be laws against what happened to that wedding cake, abandoned or not. Sure, it was sexy, good fun of the dirtiest variety but it was the kind of mistake career-minded wedding planner Lanie Malone won't repeat. At least not until next Saturday when she's once again face to face with Jason Henley, the bossy, all-trouble hotel owner who won't settle for just one night.

French Kiss- R. L. Kenderson

Jake Russo has fought for everything he's earned, and he's not about to give up the bar he's sweated over to spoiled Lacey Scott. She can kiss his ass and go back to where she flew in from. But what happens when she kisses him instead? And what if he does a lot more than kiss her back?

Irish Legend- K.C. Enders

Bartender Finn O'Meara, the self proclaimed Irish

Casanova, has met his match. He's planned everything to perfection, and he's got the girl right where he wants her. There's just one little twist - will she come around? Or is he just a legend in his own mind?

Order Sin & Tonic today

Do you love sneak peeks, book recommendations, and freebie notices? Sign up for my newsletter at www.tessalayne.com/newsletter!!

Find me on Facebook! Come on over to my house- join my ladies only Facebook group - Tessa's House. And hang on to your hat- we might get a little rowdy in there ;)

Also by Tessa Layne

PRAIRIE HEAT

PRAIRIE PASSION

PRAIRIE DESIRE

PRAIRIE STORM

PRAIRIE FIRE

PRAIRIE DEVIL

PRAIRIE FEVER

PRAIRIE REDEMPTION

PRAIRIE BLISS

A HERO'S HONOR

A HERO'S HEART

A HERO'S HAVEN

A HERO'S HOME

MR. PINK

MR. WHITE

MR. RED

MR. WHISKEY

Acknowledgments

Thank you so much for coming with me on this journey of bad boys and billionaires. I've had so much fun! More will be coming, along with more sexy alpha cowboys, firefighters, and baseball players :D

Many thanks to the Tartland Writers Association- your drinks, laughs, and encouragement mean everything.

To Swordfish Tom's- the best speakeasy in Kansas City, and the inspiration for the Whiskey Den- sans the boiler!

My heartfelt gratitude for Kara, Karin, & Erin for keeping me sane during an insane time.

And always, always to my husband. I am grateful to share every day with you